Hearts Desires and Dark Embraces

By Margaret L. Carter

Writers Exchange E-Publishing
http://www.writers-exchange.com

Hearts Desires and Dark Embraces
Copyright 2017 Margaret L. Carter
Writers Exchange E-Publishing
PO Box 372
ATHERTON QLD 4883

Cover Art by: Jatin and Sandy Cummins

Published by Writers Exchange E-Publishing
http://www.writers-exchange.com

Dedication

Dedicated to my favorite critique partner, Sandra Robinson,

Preface

When I first read *Dracula* at the age of twelve, my spontaneous reaction was to wonder how the vampire saw the events in which he was portrayed as the villain. One of my first stories, at age thirteen, was a 33-page, single-spaced saga from the viewpoint of a man in the process of transforming into a vampire. I've always found the non-human perspective, as well as relationships between human and non-human persons, fascinating.

The tales in this collection span the past ten years of my writing career. Most can be described as romances, and all involve love and passion in some form. Here you will encounter vampires, elves, ghosts, and at least one human-monster hybrid. The vampire stories in the first half of the book belong to an ongoing series based on "Vanishing Breed", a story by my husband in my first anthology, *Curse of the Undead* (1970). "Vanishing Breed" (which also appears in *Tomorrow Sucks*, edited by Greg Cox, still in print) postulates that the creatures we know as vampires belong to an alien species secretly living among us. You can get better acquainted with them in my novels, *Dark*

Changeling, *Sealed in Blood*, and *Crimson Dreams*, and two novellas, "Night Flight" and "Tall, Dark, and Deadly" (which stars Claude from "Voice from the Void").

All these stories have been previously published, except "Nursemaid", which won a fantasy award in *Romance and Beyond's* annual contest before the magazine ceased production, and "Storm of Passion", a lighthearted take on the classic horror movie scenario of being stranded for the night in a haunted house.

For more information on these and my other works, visit my website at http://www.margaretlcarter.com.

In the words of Count Dracula, "Welcome...Enter freely and of your own will!"

PART I
VAMPIRES

Voice From The Void

As the speaker stood on the tiger-skin hearth-rug droning on about hypnotism and reincarnation, Claude D'Arnot contemplated the gaslight's gleam on the man's bald head and gold-rimmed spectacles. "Recently I recovered the buried memories of a gifted subject who had served as a priestess in the temple of Dagon on the island-continent of Mu before its cataclysmic destruction..."

Claude, bored with the speech, let his eyes wander to the fur rug, complete with tail, paws, and head. His sympathies lay with the tiger, a solitary predator vastly outnumbered by both its natural prey and the human interlopers.

He shifted his attention to his own quarry, the medium, Violet, beside him on the divan. Flushing beneath his scrutiny, the young woman met his eyes for a second, then looked back at the speaker. Claude sensed Violet's skepticism--no wonder, considering her own role in the group--as well as her lack of interest in the lecture. *She's disturbed about something.* She radiated unease, reinforcing the message Claude read in her depressed skin temperature, erratic pulse, and shadowed aura.

Could this be the opening I've waited for? He'd watched her for weeks, his desire mounting, but he'd held back. He wanted more from her than a casual supper engagement. *Why? What makes this one different from any other human female?*

The medium's friend Harriet Harmon, seated on Claude's left, showed greater enthusiasm for the saga of ancient Mu, as did the other dozen or so people grouped around the drawing room. Miss Harmon leaned over to whisper in Claude's ear, "Isn't this fascinating?"

"Indeed," he murmured, waving away a maid who hovered nearby, offering a refill of his sherry.

Fascinating drivel. Among the countless people he'd mesmerized during his lifetime, not one had dropped a hint of a previous existence. But he had joined the Esoteric Order of Leviathan for entertainment, not its intellectual resources. More importantly, these occult societies made excellent hunting grounds. Women enthralled with the supernatural could easily be seduced into "ritual blood-sharing", so long as he clouded their minds to obscure the one-sided nature of the "sharing".

Claude had dabbled in several such cults, including that unsavory young fellow Crowley's circle, and the Leviathan devotees peddled the most imaginative brand of drivel he'd encountered. As far as he could untangle the threads of their doctrine, they taught that when the Elder Gods broke through from the void beyond the stars to lay waste the Earth, their faithful servants, as sole survivors, would be transformed into powerful inhuman creatures and rule the world. Those who had died before the glorious conquest would enjoy reincarnation in similarly monstrous guise. *Why not? Sounds more exciting than a cloud-paved heaven with perpetual harp music.* All the religions practiced by ephemerals struck Claude, who wavered between deism and frank agnosticism, as equally silly anyway.

A patter of applause interrupted his thoughts. The High Archon of the Order took the speaker's place in front of the hearth. "Thank you, Professor

Rinaldo, for that most enlightening presentation. That concludes the public portion of this week's convocation." He chanted a benediction in what he claimed to be ancient Sumerian. For all Claude knew, it might be; it resembled no language he'd ever heard.

The Archon, a bony middle-aged man, clean-shaven except for a bushy mustache that matched his tufted eyebrows, wore an aquamarine robe and a bronze pectoral set with semiprecious stones. A bronze circlet of similar design adorned his high forehead and abundant iron-gray hair. Though he made cryptic claims to an aristocratic bloodline, the Archon was actually a former stage magician named Matthew McFadden. Claude had satisfied his curiosity on this and other points--for instance, the medium's identity as McFadden's orphaned niece, Violet Cade--the first night they'd met, afterwards making the cult leader forget the conversation. Not that Claude disapproved of the spiritualist; as a former actor and something of a trickster himself, he could appreciate a clever charlatan.

While the maid cleared away the sherry decanters and trays of sweet biscuits, the butler ushered the guests to the front hall. Claude, along with Professor Rinaldo and Miss Harmon, had the privilege of staying for the medium's private performance, the weekly seance. During that first interview with McFadden, he'd implanted an impression of himself as a scholar of the occult who deserved a place in the Order's inner circle.

Standing, Violet said to Claude, "Will you be joining us as usual, Mr. D'Arnot?"

He heard an atypical strain in her voice. *Yes, something's bothering her tonight.* Clad in a loose, white robe, with her chestnut hair unbound, showing golden highlights in the lamp's glow, she looked ethereally delicate. Claude knew the appearance belied the facts; she managed McFadden's correspondence and financial affairs as well as any hired secretary could have. Despite her cheerful cooperation in her uncle's spiritualist schemes, in other matters she retained her innocence. Claude suspected she had no idea of the erotic symbolism of the bronze ankh pendant she wore.

Her fleeting blush, evoked by his intent gaze, stirred his appetite. He had to restrain himself from touching her by a stern reminder that he had no socially acceptable excuse for doing so.

"You know I wouldn't miss it." He said more quietly, "Miss Cade, you seem troubled. Can I help?"

Violet's aura darkened, her smile fading. "There's no need." She cast a nervous glance toward her uncle, making his farewells to the uninitiated. "There's nothing wrong."

Without directly challenging the lie, Claude whispered, "Please keep in mind, if I can offer you any assistance, simply ask."

McFadden walked over to her. "Come along, Violet. It's past time to begin the sitting."

Violet flinched, though her uncle spoke softly. "Yes, I suppose so."

I've never seen her reluctant to participate before, Claude thought. *And what has the man done to her?* His own indignation at the idea of her being hurt surprised him. *Feeling possessive about the girl already? Not a good sign.*

McFadden headed for his study, where the "sittings" took place. Rinaldo, the hypnotist, followed, with Miss Harmon close behind. She said over her shoulder to Violet, "I can't wait--this is going to be so exciting."

The medium still hung back, gazing unhappily at her friend. *So that's part of it. It's Miss Harmon's first time, and Violet has scruples about tricking her.* Claude wondered why he didn't find Harriet Harmon irresistible; traits such as her intelligence and eccentricity usually appealed to him. She made a living as a journalist, scandalous enough in itself. She wore her own version of the Bloomer costume, a long tunic over billowy trousers, which most other suffragettes had abandoned. She openly advocated free love and quoted from the poetry of Baudelaire and Swinburne. Having attended one meeting of the

Esoteric Order of Leviathan to write them up for the Society for Psychical Research, she'd lingered as, if not a convert, at least a sympathizer.

Yet Claude found himself fantasizing, instead, about Violet. He'd even begun dreaming about her. Since his kind seldom dreamed, certainly not with the sensuous clarity of the visions that had recently haunted his days, he couldn't deny how strongly the girl obsessed him. *I have to get her out of my system.* Or would this obsession yield to a night or two of dalliance? *What is it about her?* Maybe his fascination grew from the preoccupied frown with which she often stared at him, as if she saw something hidden from others. *Dangerous, if so. I ought to run the other way.*

When the group entered McFadden's study, a plump, white Persian cat with mismatched eyes, one golden and one blue, leaped down from the desk and twined around Claude's ankles. Once he had overcome her instinctive animal aversion to him, the cat, Ishtar, had become his devoted friend. He bent to stroke her while McFadden directed the others to the circular table in the center of the room. The only illumination came from a pair of tapers on the desk; according to the Archon, too much light disrupted the "astral vibrations". *With an obvious ploy like that, how does he manage to gull so many victims? And people think of our kind as rapacious!*

Besides the candles, the desk held a mummified cat, still in its tea-brown wrappings, and a green statuette about a foot high. The sculpture represented a crouching, taloned, bat-winged, tentacled figure with a vaguely humanoid visage. The table reserved for the "sitting" bore a silver chalice, with a silver-bladed dagger lying diagonally beside it, representing the feminine and masculine polarities, though of course McFadden would not be so indelicate as to make the symbolism explicit.

The occultist nodded impatiently to Claude. "Mr. D'Arnot, perhaps you'll join us so we may begin."

"Certainly, I beg your pardon." Ishtar jumped up to her usual vantage point, the top of a bookcase. Claude took his seat between Violet and Miss Harmon.

"Please join hands," McFadden commanded in his sonorous stage voice, "and remember, whatever you see or hear, do not break the circle. Discarnate entities are both sensitive and capricious. Now, we require silence for the medium's concentration. You can aid Violet's entry into trance by breathing deeply and projecting tranquility to her."

When Claude's fingers closed around Violet's slender wrist, his fingertips on the pulse point, he gave little thought to discarnate entities. The thoroughly incarnate woman at his right side held his attention, even to the exclusion of the equally healthy female on his left. The tiny hairs in his palm bristled at Violet's touch. Again he noticed that her skin was cooler than normal, and she stiffened as the others obediently relaxed into the deep-breathing exercises the leader modeled in gusty sighs. *Why this apprehension? Just because of her friend's presence? She usually treats the whole process as an entertaining charade.*

After a couple of minutes of silence, aside from the sitters' breathing, like the rush of surf on sand to Claude's sensitive ears, McFadden judged the moment ripe for a message from the "other side". Three sharp raps crackled through the air. Claude saw Rinaldo start and almost snatch his hand from McFadden's. "Good God, what was--"

"Silence!" the leader hissed. A louder rap punctuated the command.

Claude knew the origin of the noises; after the first seance he'd attended, he'd hypnotically induced McFadden to explain the tricks. The Archon wore no implements under his clothes and therefore had nothing to fear from a skeptic's search. Instead, McFadden produced the sounds by cracking his toe joints, a skill, Claude understood, possessed by many spiritualists.

"Is anyone present?" McFadden intoned.

Another minute or two of silence ensued. Claude sensed McFadden's annoyance. Violet wasn't following the script. Her fingers convulsively tightened on his. He gave her a reassuring squeeze in return.

"Is anyone here? Please reveal yourself to us. We are all sympathetic and open to your presence." A longer succession of taps.

At last Violet emitted a low moan. Her blue eyes widened in an entranced gaze that made her look almost childlike. *McFadden chose well; how could anyone suspect such an innocent maiden of fraud?* Her head rolled languidly from side to side, with parted lips and a feverish blush. Claude didn't know whether the pink tint arose naturally from her exertions or whether she was one of those rare ephemerals with some control over involuntary body functions. Either way, he enjoyed the effect.

"Yes, speak to us," McFadden said. "Do not be afraid. Span the gulf between this world and the next, and appear before us."

More raps. Another moan from the medium. A glowing vapor began to coalesce above the center of the table. Both Rinaldo and Miss Harmon gasped. Claude had to admit he'd been impressed, too, when he'd first seen the phosphorescent cloud. McFadden produced it by stepping on a trigger underneath the Oriental carpet, activating a device inside the table. For the "ectoplasm" he had to rely on mechanical aids, risking discovery, but so far no observer had insisted on peeling up the carpet or dismantling the furniture. McFadden did have in his favor the conspicuous absence of the cabinet most physical mediums used; his seance room looked like a respectable gentleman's study.

"Who is there? Do you have a message for one of our number?"

Violet gave a hollow groan. *Why isn't she delivering the message, whatever that may be?*

"Speak, we await you," said McFadden. Even the other ephemerals, Claude reflected, should sense his impatience.

"Rinaldo," Violet sighed. The hypnotist jerked up his head. "Your work--" She exhaled a long breath, as if drawing the words from a deep well. "Sophia is here. She is watching over your work."

"Sophia! Oh, my God!"

"Who is she?" said McFadden in a soft, solicitous voice.

"My daughter--died twelve years ago--fifteen years old."

McFadden had known that, of course. Like any confidence man, the occultist had his sources. He passed on the relevant information to Violet and coached her in its use.

The Archon said, "Please be quiet, Professor, lest you disrupt the ether."

"Sophia is well--happy--" Violet murmured.

That's what paying customers want to hear, Claude thought. Not that the Archon would be so crass to ask for money, but grateful mourners never failed to make donations to the Order. If they didn't do so spontaneously, the "spirits" dropped hints. Claude couldn't fathom this fad for believing that, while waiting to reincarnate, the dead hovered at the beck and call of "sensitives" like astral parlormaids. *Well, maybe they do; what do I know about the post-mortem destiny of ephemerals?*

Violet continued, "Your work brings great comfort to many. But take care with your gifts, lest you unleash powers beyond your ken."

Good advice for anyone dabbling in mesmerism, but judging from McFadden's frown, not what he'd instructed her to say.

She finished with, "Sophia watches over you and waits to rejoin you in the next incarnation. Be of good cheer." She slumped in her chair, miming exhaustion from the strain of the otherworldly powers surging through her.

The phosphorescent mist thickened, coalescing over the table like steam from a teakettle until each face was shrouded in an eerie, bluish-green veil. More cracklings and poppings sounded.

"Someone else is here," said McFadden. "Speak, we are listening!"

Violet gave a loud groan. Claude felt her hand quivering with tension.

"Yes, Violet, open yourself to the higher plane. Let the spirits emerge from the void beyond this world and deliver their message through you."

"Harriet Harmon," she breathed.

"Yes? You have a communication for Miss Harmon?"

That lady leaned forward, trying to peer around Claude at Violet without breaking their handclasp.

"Your father--"

Claude felt Miss Harmon go rigid. Her father, he knew, had died four years previously. "Is he there?" she whispered.

Instead of answering, Violet threw back her head and writhed in her chair, as if fighting an invasion from beyond. The undulations of her slender body in the soft robe impressed Claude as blatantly erotic. *Does she know that? Probably not; she's too upset about her friend.*

"Do not resist the power," said McFadden. "Let the departed one speak through your mouth."

The medium let out a wail and collapsed, face down. Claude knew she wasn't unconscious, but Rinaldo and Miss Harmon accepted the "faint" as real.

Scowling in unconcealed disgust, McFadden stood. "Some hostile elemental is doubtless blocking the vibrations." He turned up the gaslight. "I apologize, Miss Harmon, for leaving you in suspense, but the spirits cannot be coerced."

"Never mind. It's Violet I'm concerned about." She propped up the medium, patting her face. "Someone ring for smelling salts."

Violet's eyes fluttered open. "No, that's all right. I'm fine now. I only need to rest." Between them, Claude and Miss Harmon helped her to her feet.

Effective performance, Claude thought, *and if I were being threatened with a whiff of ammonia, I'd have a miraculous recovery, too.*

"Violet should be fully recuperated by tomorrow night," said McFadden with a pointed stare at his niece. "Miss Harmon, if you'll return then, we can hold a private sitting for you. Perhaps the spirits will become more amenable." The anger simmering behind his solemn facade made Claude's nerves itch.

"I'd be very grateful." She patted her friend's shoulder. "Are you quite certain--?"

"I'm perfectly well. You go home now." Violet cast a look of silent appeal at Claude. He responded with a minute nod, wishing he could answer more openly.

McFadden rang for the butler to show out the guests.

Claude, bringing up the rear, cornered the butler in the foyer and said, "I left at the same time as the others. You may as well lock up for the night."

With an unwary subject, imprinting a false memory took no more effort than that. As soon as the servant's back was turned, Claude's presence forgotten, Claude invoked a psychic shield that shrouded him from human sight. Although a mirror or a kodak print would show his image, and animals could sense his presence, to human eyes he was virtually invisible.

He had no trouble finding McFadden and Violet. The man's angry shouts echoed through the house. With the cat, Ishtar, padding at his heels, Claude followed the noise to a closed door. When he eased it open, Ishtar slipped in ahead of him.

Violet, sitting on a divan in a stuffy parlor redolent of stale cigars, blinked at the sight of the door moving "by itself". Apparently deciding, though, that the cat had caused the phenomenon, she returned her gaze to her uncle.

McFadden loomed over her, his back to the entrance. "What's got into you, ye gormless chit?" A Scottish burr, usually disguised by his stage mannerisms, roughened his voice. "Why did ye not say the lines I gave you?"

"I won't do that to Harriet." Though her voice shook, she folded her arms and glared at him.

"I'm the master of this house! It's not your place to say what ye will and will not do!" He made an effort to rein his anger, though his aura still smoldered a dull red. "Come, lass, ye had no such quibbles all the other times."

"Harriet is my friend. I won't trick her out of money she can't spare or wring her heart with 'messages' from her dead father."

"Don't tell me what ye won't do! I've fed, clothed, and sheltered you these fifteen years. I have a right to some gratitude."

Violet sprang to her feet. "Gratitude doesn't go that far! I think I've repaid you more than--"

McFadden grabbed her shoulders and shook her. "Hold your peace while I'm speaking to you!"

She gave a choked gasp. On a table behind her, a tall vase vibrated momentarily, then toppled to the floor.

What was that? Claude wondered. *The cat? I don't see--*

He was distracted by a surge of fear from McFadden, accompanied by a hoarse shout. "Damn you, ye'll do as ye're told!" McFadden slapped Violet across the mouth.

Enough! Claude seized him and spun him around. Violet emitted a soft cry as Claude's psychic veil dissolved, rendering him visible. Only the fear in her eyes stopped him from hitting McFadden. *And a good thing, too; I would probably break his neck.*

"Listen to me, you worthless--" He couldn't think of an epithet that wouldn't shock Violet even worse. His eyes impaled McFadden's. "You will not strike your niece again. You will treat her with courtesy at all times. Now go to bed, and forget you saw me."

He shoved the occultist toward the door. McFadden hustled into the corridor.

When the sound of the man's footsteps faded up the stairs, Claude turned toward Violet, perched on the edge of the divan. She trembled, and the normal rosy glow of her aura was dimmed.

He sat beside her and took her hand before she could shrink from him. "Please don't be afraid, *ma petite*." He succumbed to the temptation to kiss her fingertips. "Everything is perfectly all right."

She stared at him intently. "I'm not afraid now. But I never saw you come in." That puzzled frown reappeared.

What does she see when she looks at me that way? "Don't worry about that." He stood up, still holding her hand. "Walk with me in the garden. I want to talk to you."

When she hesitated, he encouraged her with a gentle psychic caress, light as the brush of a feather. She nodded.

They met no servants on their way, emerging into the garden through the French doors of a back sitting room. The house, a Queen Anne style mansion bookended by red brick chimneys and liberally studded with gables, lay on the outskirts of London. It enjoyed the convenience of closeness to the city while avoiding the noise, the stink of garbage and horse droppings, and the sooty reek of the ubiquitous yellow fog. Instead, white roses festooning a nearby trellis perfumed the summer night air.

On the graveled path, Claude offered Violet his arm. Her body heat warmed him like a roaring fire in midwinter. He longed to draw her into an embrace, but in her agitated condition, he would have to override her will, an act he wanted to avoid. *I don't want her as prey; I want her for a pet.*

The thought stunned him. *So that is what's the matter with me!* He was bored with entranced victims; he craved a donor who could accept him with a clear mind, fully aware of his nature and his needs--as much as he chose to reveal. With unwitting prey, he didn't dare resort to a given donor more than once or twice. He obtained most of his modest but necessary doses of human blood (a supplement to the staple diet drained from horses, rats, and stray dogs) from music hall dancers and ladies of the evening. *With Violet, it could be different.* And in her case, he wanted to offer something in return for the vital fluid and psychic energy he feasted upon.

Something besides pleasure. That aspect went without saying. He sensed desire in the rise of her skin temperature, heard it in the quickening of her breath and heartbeat, even if propriety wouldn't allow her to recognize her own passion. The previous century, the time of Claude's youth, had taken a more sensible attitude toward the mating dance; a human male of that era would have guffawed at the notion that women felt no sexual impulses.

Well, before he could consider seducing Violet, he had to settle this problem with her uncle. "Miss Cade--may I call you Violet? After tonight, we needn't stand on formality, need we?"

"I suppose not--Claude." She swayed closer to him, her fingers tightening on his sleeve. For a second, he felt lightheaded.

Not now, he chastised himself. "Tell me about that argument with your uncle."

"Harriet has a small annual income, inherited from her father, enough to live on. That's why she can afford to write for the few newspapers that'll use her work--she doesn't earn enough to support herself. Not yet, anyway."

"And McFadden wants to get his hooks into that money, of course." They reached a stream rippling at the bottom of the garden. Claude guided Violet to a marble bench under a willow tree. "Forgive me for sounding like him, but why were you willing to play similar tricks on his other guests?"

"True, it wasn't honest," she said, "but it always seemed like a game to me. They're all rich people, or at least prosperous. I tell them what they want to hear, and Uncle Matthew never takes more than they can afford to lose--just a drop in the bucket, in most cases. He really isn't greedy."

Claude couldn't repress a derisive laugh.

"Really," she said. "He could have robbed them blind--some fake spiritualists do. I keep his books, so I know he isn't taking half the advantage he could."

"But it's different with Miss Harmon."

"I'm having second thoughts about the others, too. Poor Professor Rinaldo--" Violet shook her head. "But especially Harriet. I quarreled with Uncle Matthew about that earlier. Harriet's my friend. I can't lie to her, not when she joined the Order in good faith, out of scientific curiosity. And she *can't* afford to throw away money on Uncle Matthew's cult. She needs it to live on. What little she can spare, she donates to suffragist societies."

Claude cupped her right hand in both of his. "Why don't you simply leave your uncle? Is it money?"

She sighed. "You must think me awfully mercenary."

"Not at all. Please continue."

"That's exactly what Harriet thinks I should do, and she doesn't even know that, as a medium, I'm a fraud. She's invited me to move into her flat, but I can't live off her. I have no money of my own, not yet, anyway. Uncle Matthew has control of my inheritance until I turn thirty, and I'm only twenty-six." When Claude made no comment, she said, "Oh, it's easy enough to say I should earn my own living, but what skills do I have?"

"Granted," he said, "respectable employment agencies probably have few positions open for mediums."

She laughed at that, and her aura brightened. "I suppose I could become a governess or factory girl. Both of those choices sound awfully grim. Harriet suggested I write a book about my experiences with spiritualism. She doesn't know it would have to be an exposure of fraud, and I don't want to do that to Uncle Matthew, whatever his flaws."

Claude swallowed the impatient retort that sprang to mind. "Surely you don't agree with his self-serving argument that you 'owe' him."

"He did take me in when my parents died of scarlet fever," she said. "It couldn't have been easy for him, dealing with a girl of eleven. He *has* fed, sheltered, and clothed me all these years."

"Yes, compensated by free access to your trust fund!"

"Remember, I keep his accounts. I'm not completely naive. I would have noticed if he'd skimmed off an excessive amount. And even though he's harsh sometimes, he's never really hurt me."

"Oh, barring the occasional slap?" At her blank look, Claude decided not to pursue the issue. Ephemerals routinely "disciplined" their young in ways "lower" animals wouldn't dream of. "Forgive me for asking, but has he ever--" *What's the currently acceptable euphemism?* "Does he--interfere with you?"

"Oh, no!" Her astonished tone and hot blush convinced Claude of her sincerity. "Uncle Matthew was very patient with me when I first came to live with him. He didn't have this house then. He bought it a few years ago, when he started to make money. He lived in a small cottage, so it must have been even harder on him."

"Why? I can't imagine you as a difficult child." Sensing her reluctance to answer, he gave her another mental nudge.

She drew a deep breath. "Things--objects--flew through the air. It only started after I moved in with him." She gave Claude an appealing glance. "I hope you don't think I'm lying or mad."

So that explains the falling vase. "Certainly not. I've heard of such phenomena."

"At that time, I hadn't. I was frightened out of my wits. I thought the cottage was haunted. So did the housekeeper--she gave notice after the first week." Violet giggled. "It wasn't funny then. Next, I thought *I* was haunted. Uncle Matthew helped me get over my fears. Until he coaxed me out of it, I was sure I was possessed by a devil. Sometimes I still wonder." A shiver coursed through her. "That was what gave him the idea of training me as a medium. He was terribly disappointed that I couldn't make it happen on command. Then, after a couple of years, the whole thing stopped."

"Fascinating," said Claude. *She doesn't realize the power still lies locked inside her mind.* When he paused to reflect on the details, he had to choke down a snarl. "That bloody--pardon me, your uncle--used you in his confidence games when you were a mere child?"

Violet shrugged. "I was twelve when we started. It was better than slaving away like Jane Eyre. And as I said, I've always thought of it as a game. I was good at it. It helps that I can see--something--a halo of colored light around living things. Uncle Matthew calls it the etheric body."

Claude nodded. *She can actually see the aura?*

"I can use that to pick up people's feelings and adjust my spirit messages to fit."

"Indeed?" Excitement tingled up Claude's spine, along with a whisper of danger that he ignored. "I've never met anyone who can perceive--etheric bodies." *No one human, that is.*

She gazed intently at him, though she couldn't have discerned details in the moonlight. "You do believe me, don't you?"

"Of course."

"I'm so glad. I don't dare talk about it, not to ordinary people outside spiritualist circles. They'd think I was out of my mind."

"I know you aren't." He put his arm around her shoulders, and she leaned against him instead of drawing away. The flutter of her pulse made his throat go dry.

"I shouldn't be surprised that you'd understand. The first time we met, I noticed how different your--halo--is."

"In what way?" *So that's why she keeps staring at me.*

"It's unique. I've never seen another one like it--streaked with velvet black and a sort of iridescent blue-violet."

"Interesting observation." *Is it safe to have her noticing that? Confound it, I don't care!* Now he knew why she enticed him. She sensed his difference, as few human females could. "And poetically phrased. Perhaps you *should* write a book."

"I already told you--"

"That you don't want to expose your uncle--though your reasoning still eludes me. But you don't have to. Join the Society for Psychical Research and use your background to expose other charlatans. Write novels based on your outre experiences. Live with your friend Miss Harmon and become a celebrated author."

She laughed at that but quickly sobered. "It sounds wonderful--once I get past the ordeal of explaining to Harriet that I'm a fake--but Uncle Matthew wouldn't let me go without a fight. It's not only the money--I know his secrets. And you've distracted me from the main problem. What about that seance he's planning for tomorrow night?"

"Leave that to me. I've acted onstage, and I have some skill in mesmerism." Both claims were true, though far from the whole truth. "You just make up with your uncle and convince him you've had a change of heart about tomorrow's performance. Then go into your trance act, put on a dramatic display of writhing and chanting--rather like the Delphic Oracle--and trust me for the rest. No matter how strange it may appear."

"What are you going to do?"

"It would be complicated to explain, and I prefer your reaction to be spontaneous." In fact, he wanted to leave matters vague in case she reacted so negatively that he had to erase her memory. "McFadden will know the--phenomena--I'll create aren't part of his own bag of tricks, and he won't realize I'm there. After the peculiar things that happened in your girlhood, he shouldn't be hard to convince that you have unplumbed occult depths. I plan to frighten him so thoroughly he'll give you whatever you demand and leave you alone afterward."

She shook her head. "It sounds quite incredible to me. But I do trust you--Claude."

Stroking her hair, he tilted her face toward him and lightly kissed her parted lips. She drew in a startled breath that, along with the fragrance of her skin, almost wrecked his fragile self-restraint.

Tomorrow night, damn it! This time I'll earn my reward before I take it. If he planned to treat her as a pet rather than a victim, he ought to practice adhering to human ethical standards. *How else can I be honest with her? Or as honest as the situation permits, anyway.*

The next evening, Claude rode a hansom cab to McFadden's and ordered the driver to wait at a bend in the road just out of sight of the house. As soon as Claude was sure the cabby could no longer see him, he shrouded himself. Invisible to human eyes, he lurked near the front door until Harriet Harmon arrived, then glided inside with her.

Moments later, he was ensconced in the study, leaning against the bookcase, the psychic veil still intact. Ishtar, of course, knew of his presence. She rubbed against his trousers and meowed up at him with an insistence that would convince any susceptible observer of a ghostly presence. Petting her, he hushed her with a silent command. With an insulted flick of her plumed tail, she jumped onto her customary shelf.

McFadden escorted Violet and Harriet to their places at the circular table. "The astral energies are perfectly balanced tonight," he said. "I feel it. Don't you agree, Violet?"

Noting the occultist's imperious glower at Violet, Claude had to remind himself that ripping off the man's head would spoil the plan.

"Yes, I'm certain of it." Violet surveyed the study, obviously wondering how Claude could appear out of the woodwork in a room ostentatiously devoid of hiding places. He wished he could somehow reassure her.

"Then let us begin." The three of them joined hands and commenced the breathing exercises that supposedly cleared the channels for energies from the void beyond the earthly plane.

Claude waited for the spirit rappings with which McFadden always began the performance. They duly occurred within three or four minutes. *Isn't he getting a trifle too predictable? Without Violet's talent, he'll wear out his repertoire in short order. He knows how much he needs her; that must be why he's controlling her so harshly.*

"Is someone attempting to break through from the other side?" McFadden intoned. "Come forward and speak through the vessel prepared for you."

Violet emitted a keening cry. On cue, McFadden's foot pressed the button concealed under the carpet. Claude noticed the minute tension in the man's body and watched for his next reaction. When the phosphorescent cloud didn't appear, McFadden scowled at Violet, who lolled in her chair with eyes half closed, moaning. In the moment or two before the others had entered, Claude had gouged a tiny hole in the rug and disconnected the device.

McFadden, of course, likely thought Violet had sabotaged him, but he couldn't give away his own trick by accusing her in front of Harriet. Smoothing over his expression, he continued, "Emerge from the void and speak to us! What message do you bear this night?"

Shrieking as if in agony, Violet went rigid, then shook all over like a woman in a *grand mal* seizure. McFadden fixed her with a dubious stare, obviously not quite sure her paroxysm wasn't genuine.

Well done, thought Claude. *Better not drag this out any further.*

He projected a silent signal to the cat. Ishtar executed a flying leap from the bookshelf to the center of the table, knocking over the empty chalice. Face to face with McFadden, she screamed as if plunged into boiling water.

McFadden sprang to his feet, overturning his chair. Ishtar stopped yowling and vented a drawn-out hiss. Claude charged toward the occultist, simultaneously replacing his psychic shield with a new illusion, based on the green statuette on the desk, that he'd spent the last few minutes visualizing. At the instant he materialized from nowhere, he cloaked himself in an image of vast, dark wings, hawklike talons, blazing eyes, fangs, and a shadowy suggestion of tentacles. At least, that was what he aimed for, and McFadden's terror confirmed the success of the ploy.

McFadden raised his hands before his face and gibbered.

Claude dug his nails into the man's shoulders and roared, "Puny mortal, do not meddle in affairs beyond your ken! Forbear to call up what you cannot put down!" The words reverberated around the small room like echoes in a cavern.

McFadden replied with a wordless cry of panic. Claude heard screams from the two women but couldn't break his illusion to console them.

"Cease this blasphemy, lest worse befall you!"

He decided he'd better vanish before McFadden, with his own experience in similar deception, recovered enough to think rationally.

To Claude's surprise, though, the occultist lunged for the table and snatched up the dagger. "Fiend! Begone to Hell! *Retro me, Sathanas!*" He stabbed wildly into the spectral, flame-eyed, bat-winged monster he saw before him.

Dark Powers, he believes that nonsense about silver! Silver or not, it didn't matter; with all his energy focused on the illusion, his external form in flux, Claude was almost as vulnerable to the weapon as an ordinary man. When the blade drove into his shoulder, pain slammed through him. As the attacker pulled it free, Claude felt as if a shaft of ice pierced him to the heart.

Behind him, Violet cried, "No!"

On the desk, the green carving of the winged, tentacled idol rose into the air. It sailed across the room, gaining speed with every inch, and collided with McFadden's skull. He collapsed face down across the table.

Claude, his vision clearing as he dropped the illusion and struggled to bring the pain under control, slumped into the nearest vacant chair. The sound of hurrying footsteps penetrated his awareness.

He gestured weakly to Violet. "Servants--don't let them in."

To her credit, Violet collected herself enough to open the door a crack at the butler's knock. His worried voice mumbled an inquiry. "There's nothing wrong," she told him in a surprisingly steady tone. "I'm sorry for the disturbance. It's only one of Uncle Matthew's experiments. You may retire."

Harriet, standing beside the table, cast frantic glances at McFadden and Claude. *Can't let her start asking questions. Bloody hell, I'm too tired for this.* And in a few minutes, when the shock wore off, thirst would ravage him. Well, he could use that; the need enhanced his mesmeric power. "Harriet," he whispered.

She looked straight at him. He captured her gaze and spoke more firmly, "Violet is right. This was only an experiment, a trick. No harm has been done. Go home at once, and forget the details of what just happened. It's nothing to be concerned about. Nothing but stage magic. You understand?"

Harriet nodded. "I'll go home now." She turned to Violet with a bewildered frown. "Violet?"

"I'm perfectly well. I'll call on you as soon as I can."

With another hesitant nod, Harriet groped for the door like a sleepwalker and disappeared down the hall. Fortunately she drove her own pony chaise, even at night (another unladylike habit), so she would have no difficulty getting home.

Violet shut the door and turned on Claude. "I didn't ask you to kill him!"

"He isn't dead, only stunned. And I did *not* do that."

"Then what--"

"We'd better discuss it elsewhere." He'd managed to suppress most of the pain but couldn't concentrate well enough to eliminate all of it. As for self-healing, he could do no more than stop the bleeding. He needed a quiet, safe refuge--and nourishment. "I strongly suggest we get out before he wakes up."

"How--"

"I have a cab waiting. Come home with me. Yes, unchaperoned--at this point, does that really worry you? As soon as I'm sure you'll be all right, I'll send you to Miss Harmon's."

"Very well." After lighting the gas, she bent over her uncle and felt for the pulse at his wrist. "You're right, he's alive. Are you certain it's safe to leave him like this?"

"He'll recover." Although McFadden's scalp oozed blood--the scent made Claude's jaws ache--his aura showed that he'd suffered no permanent damage.

When Claude stood up and reached for Violet's hand, she focused on him for the first time. "You're wounded, too! He stabbed you!"

"It's nothing. It's already stopped bleeding." Violet had no way of knowing how serious the wound would have been for an ordinary man. He forestalled further conversation by grasping her arm and guiding her out of the study, closing the door behind them.

The night air energized him enough to make the walk to the waiting hansom less of an ordeal than he'd feared. After giving directions to the driver, Claude settled into the seat with an audible sigh. He didn't mind displaying his exhaustion to Violet now.

"You *are* hurt. We'll have to get a doctor."

"Absolutely not." He gazed at her, knowing she would see a glint of crimson in his eyes. After what he'd already shown her, that would scarcely drive her into hysterics. "It was worth it, *ma petite*. Your uncle will be well and truly convinced that you can 'call spirits from the vasty deep'. After that message from the void, he wouldn't dare deny you anything you ask."

Violet gathered her wits and managed a smile. "What shall I ask?"

"Strike while the iron is hot, before he has time to rationalize the experience. Tomorrow morning, send for your personal effects, and order him to contact his solicitor about transferring your funds into your control."

"You think he'll listen?"

"If he doesn't," said Claude with a feral grin, "I'll have a talk with him. But he will. You saw him go after me with that knife, silver for demons. He *believed*."

She stared hard at him. In the dim interior of the cab, she could only be examining his aura. "That statuette--if you didn't make it fly at him, then who--"

"That's obvious. You did. Just as you made that vase break earlier."

"No! I told you, I've never been able to--"

"Do it voluntarily? Perhaps not, but you did it under the stress of strong emotion. And now that you know you haven't lost the power, you may be able to train yourself to duplicate the feat." *No wonder she attracts me. Ephemerals with psychic talents of their own make the best donors.*

"For what?" she said. "I'm retiring as a medium, remember?"

"Research for those novels you plan to write."

She lightly touched his hand. The motion of the carriage made her sway against him. His head reeled at the tantalizing sensation of her warm skin, the blood throbbing in her fingertips.

"Should I research you for my novels, too, Claude?"

"What do you mean?" *How much can she infer on her own? And how much do I dare let her comprehend?*

"Don't insult my intelligence! I've known all along that you were--different--because of those odd colors in your etheric body. I just never suspected how different! What I saw in there *wasn't* simple hypnotism, and it certainly wasn't stage magic. What kind of man are you?" She gulped. "Are you even human?"

His need made him reckless. *Oh, the Devil take it, if this turns out badly, I can revise her memory later.* "Let me show you."

Putting an arm around her shoulders, he lifted her hand to his lips. He flicked his tongue in butterfly caresses over the palm down to the wrist. Violet's quiver of response had nothing to do with fear. Tilting his head, he used the razor-edge of his incisors to open a tiny incision--he had no fangs like the monsters in those absurd penny-dreadfuls. While he lapped the trickle of blood, she leaned into his embrace, her breath rapid and shallow.

Claude forced himself to stop long before he'd had enough. He allowed her to see him slowly lick the droplets from his lips.

Applying pressure to the cut, he said, "I'll take no more without your free consent."

She gaped at him for a minute before collecting her wits to speak. "Are you a--one of those--creatures--in Mr. Stoker's latest novel?"

Good Lord, how long is that tripe going to haunt us? With any luck, that idiotic book will fade into the oblivion it deserves before the year's out. Well, at least she isn't screaming in terror.

"Mr. Stoker's novel is a pack of bloody half-truths and damned lies!" He winced at the pain his incautious outburst reawakened. "Forgive my language. We feel very strongly about the way we've been libeled."

"Then it isn't true about--I won't become like you?"

"*Ma petite*, I am neither a walking corpse nor contagious. I'm as much a part of the natural world as you are." He decided to withhold further specifics until they'd become intimate.

She held up her hand near the window, trying to examine the minute wound in the moonlight. "This certainly isn't much like the book. Don't you need--have you had enough?" She blushed, obviously recalling her own arousal.

"I've expended energy, not lost a large amount of blood, so what I need is quality, not fluid volume. However, your intuition is correct--that wasn't enough."

He gently brushed his fingers over the bodice of her ceremonial robe, feeling her nipples tighten under the thin fabric. Her breath caught, but she didn't object. Virginal as she was, she would need little more than that caress and his mouth at her throat to bring her to fulfillment.

She offered her right wrist again. "Go ahead, then. I'm not afraid."

"Yes, you are, a bit. Anyone would be. But you needn't. It gets much better." He kissed her hand without grazing the cut.

"I'm not sure how I feel about serving as--well--food."

"Oh, no, my dear, if it were only that, I wouldn't even let you be aware of what I'm doing. You would enjoy it in a trance and forget immediately. You aren't a victim--you are my natural complement."

Her brow creased in puzzlement.

"That psychic talent of yours," he reminded her.

"I still doubt I could levitate objects on purpose."

"Why don't you try?"

"Now?"

"Certainly. I want to settle all your doubts before we--share--again." He removed his signet ring and laid it on her lap. "Go ahead."

She stared at the ring for more than a minute. "It's no use. I haven't the slightest idea how to begin."

"Let me help." He cupped her chin, turned her head toward him, and gazed into her eyes. "Relax, let your inner strength flow freely. All the power you need lies within you."

When he released her, she shifted her eyes to the ring, and it floated two feet into the air as smoothly as if raised by an invisible wire.

She gasped in delighted astonishment, and the object fell to the floor of the carriage. Picking it up, she said, "Are you sure you didn't do that yourself?"

"I'm not capable of it. You have my word."

She gave him a vigorous hug. "And all these years I was afraid--thinking I'd been possessed by some evil force, that might attack me again--and it was under my control all the time!"

Her vital heat made his teeth tingle in anticipation. *Not in a cab, damn it!* "Ease off--my self-control isn't what it should be at the moment." He untwined her arms from his neck and moved a few inches away from her. "We'll arrive at my townhouse in a minute or two." *And not a moment too soon!* "Then, if you're willing--"

Her aura scintillated in harmony with her smile. "To 'share'? That sounds like a most intriguing way to start my new life."

(Story originally published in *The Time Of The Vampires*, ed. P. N. Elrod and Martin Greenberg, DAW, 1996)

The Pale Hill's Side

Do elves feel the cold on chilly nights?

Judith McCrae tugged her thin shawl tighter around her shoulders. She'd forgotten how cool the Yorkshire downs could become after sunset on the last day of April. Critically examining her sketch of the beehive-shaped mound some fifty yards distant, she smiled at the fancy that a faerie lord might emerge from beneath the earth to carry her off. Even the country people who still called these prehistoric structures "elf-mounds" knew better; after all, the dawn of the twentieth century was only three years away.

Nevertheless, none of the locals approached this part of the moor after dark. Too many cattle had been found dead here, with no visible wounds. The rumors reminded Judith of the folk belief that elves drained milk from cows by night.

As an avid reader of Mr. Yeats' collections of Irish fairy tales, she couldn't resist making a detour in her holiday to investigate this reputedly elf-haunted site. Especially on May Eve, a very appropriate night. Now, though, the chill was quenching her enthusiasm.

The boy who'd guided her here had long since run home to bed. Judith was almost ready to do the same; she would have a tedious hike back to the village. Sketching the mound by moonlight had certainly filled her mind with enough "atmosphere" to render an intriguing article on north country superstitions that might earn her a few pounds.

The boy, Robbie--sadness shadowed her at the memory of his thin, pale face. Only fourteen years old, and unlikely to live to fifteen. As a doctor's daughter, Judith recognized the early signs of consumption in his pallor and his constant cough. His eyes had glimmered with tears and longing when he'd told her how he'd wandered here just two nights before. An elven lord, he said, had appeared on the moor and bespelled him. When Judith had asked Robbie to describe this being, the boy had stammered into awed silence. "Silver fire," was all he could say. He'd yearned to follow the elf-lord into the mound, but the creature had given him one burning touch and sent him away.

"He said I was too sickly, Miss." Robbie longed to see the creature again and would have lingered with Judith if she hadn't given him a handful of coins and ordered him to go home.

Suppressing a shiver from a gust of wind, Judith closed her sketchpad and picked up the electric torch that lay beside her on the blanket. Time to start back. As she stood up, stretching her stiff limbs, a movement caught her eye. A flicker of shadow between her and the mound.

She took a deep breath to tame the racing of her heart. What nonsense-- she didn't believe in fairies. These barrows were nothing but the desolate tombs of prehistoric men. She scanned the dark slopes of the hilly moor, broken by outcroppings of rock barely visible in the moonlight. *Next I'll be seeing the ghost of Heathcliff. No more Bronte romances at bedtime, Miss Judith!*

Her fingers tightened on the torch. The sooner she returned to the inn, the better. While supernatural menaces sprang from over-fertile imagination, the real danger of robbers--or worse--might stalk here.

Having an attack of the vapors, now? she chided herself. She turned her back on the barrow and knelt to fold the blanket.

A man appeared in front of her.

He didn't appear out of thin air! It's impossible! She didn't waste time arguing with herself. Dropping everything she held, she made a sideways dash.

And nearly collided with him.

She looked up--looked upward forever, it seemed; she'd never seen so tall a man--into eyes that gleamed silver. He didn't let her run again. Cold fingers closed on her wrist.

Her attempt to struggle died stillborn. She felt dizzy. *So Robbie wasn't spinning an idle tale.* A line from Coleridge came into her head: "His flashing eyes, his floating hair--"

She was floating, and the man's--the elf's--face floated above her. *Of course, he's carrying me.* By the time she realized this fact, they had passed into the mound. Her panic flowed away like ice melting in a spring thaw. Instead, she accepted her helplessness with a dreamy languor. "Though I am old with wandering, through hollow lands and hilly lands--" That was Yeats. Judith felt a drowsy satisfaction at finding herself immersed in an adventure one of the foremost poets of the decade could only imagine.

When she forced her eyes away from the elf's to look at the tunnel around her, it seemed the walls shimmered as if made of water rather than rock. Or living jewels. She was carried through rainbow-hued curtains. Whether they parted before her captor, or he slipped through like a ghost, she couldn't tell.

After an immeasurable time, he set her on her feet. "You can walk from here, I trust." His voice made her diaphragm quiver, as the bass note of an organ might. Yet she heard something less unearthly behind it, a hint of a Scottish burr.

Hearing him speak cleared her head a little. She let him take her hand and lead her along the path between the glowing walls. Did his touch chill or burn? She couldn't focus clearly enough to decide. "What do you want with me?"

"My sister's child was wounded by one of your people's weapons. You are here for healing."

Elves can be hurt? Why don't they just work a bit of magic? she wondered muzzily. "Then you need a doctor, not me." Dimly she recalled Robbie's tale of rejection. "I won't be much more use than that boy you met the other night."

"That isn't the kind of help we require." She felt his eyes upon her. "Have you never heard that the Fair Folk abduct human nurses to feed their children?"

That doesn't make sense. I'm not a mother. Never even--

Led by the elf-lord, she emerged into a vaulted chamber whose walls glittered from the flames of numerous candles. "Is this sufficient light for you?" he asked. "It's far more than we need."

Judith nodded. Her eyes took in a confused impression of hundreds of books, silken wall hangings, and a wide bed with a tall, slender woman standing next to it.

"Fiona, I've brought you one that should serve well enough."

As he led Judith toward the bed, the elven woman stepped to meet them. For the first time Judith paused for a good look at her captor. His long hair made a dark halo around his pale, sharp-featured face. His sister had the same silver eyes, glowing with pinpoints of red at the centers, and the same hair so black it gleamed, except that hers hung to her waist and seemed to ripple in an unfelt breeze when she moved. Both wore shining garments with capes that fanned behind them at every step.

In a moment of clarity Judith thought, *It's too perfect, too much like the poets' tales and my own daydreams.*

Renewed dizziness overcame her when the elf-lady's nails grazed her chin. "A fine choice, Tammas," said the woman. "Shall we get on with it?"

Tammas? Fiona? These are Faerie names?

As if Judith had spoken her doubts aloud, the male elf said, "We borrow names from the folk we dwell among. Come, we've no time to waste." He drew her to the bedside.

She gazed down at a pale, thin child of ten or twelve, by human reckoning. The unconscious body was covered to the waist, the exposed parts naked. From the flat chest, delicate features, and wispy, golden red, shoulder-length hair, Judith couldn't tell whether the creature was male or female. But her gaze didn't linger on the sharp nose and chin or the feathery lashes of the closed eyes. She stifled a gasp at the sight of the unbandaged bullet wound on the left side of the ribcage.

"Shot? When?"

"Two nights ago." Tammas didn't look at her as he answered. He was leaning over the child, his hands stroking the temples.

More than half-awake now, Judith contemplated the injury. In two nights, without treatment, how could the wound have closed so far already? On the other hand, considering how bad it must have been when it was fresh, how could the child have survived at all? What could elves--she was aware enough now to realize the incongruity, the impossibility, of this situation--know of medicine? Had they even removed the bullet?

Again answering her unspoken thoughts, the elf-lord said, "We performed what--surgery--was required. The rest only you, or someone like you, can provide." His fingertips resting on the child's forehead, he crooned, "Wake. You are safe."

Violet-gray eyes fluttered open. They drifted to Judith's face. The floating sensation washed over her again. She faintly heard Tammas' voice saying, "She is for you, Liam." She felt Tammas' chill grasp as he guided her hand to the center of the child's chest.

Liam? It's a boy, then. Though she felt no heartbeat, she knew from the awakening glow in the creature's eyes that life smoldered in him. The glow lured her closer. She stretched out on the bed and wrapped her arms around the elf-child. Icy fingers explored her hair and the nape of her neck. Enfolded in darkness, she heard inside her head the crashing of waves on a stony shore. Their rhythm lulled her into nothingness.

The glow. It's still here. When her eyes focused, Judith realized she was staring, not at eyes of unearthly beauty, but at a kerosene lantern. *Merciful Heaven, what a dream!*

When she sat up, she groaned aloud at the aches in her stiff limbs. Beneath her lay a pallet on a smooth rock surface. Bare rock walls surrounded her. *Oh, God, not a dream!* Some of the night's strangeness, at least, had been real; she was a prisoner underground.

Shivering, her eyes gritty from sleep, she surveyed her cell. The chamber was about ten feet in diameter, its entrance covered by a heavy scarlet drape. Beside her "bed" sat a neat stack of objects--blanket, sketchpad, pencils--all the possessions she'd left on the moor, even the electric torch. A few feet away she saw a tall pitcher, basin, and tumbler of earthenware, a plate, and a chamberpot. The atmosphere was musty but not suffocating; crevices overhead must admit some air.

Fighting both her fear and the pain in her chilled muscles, she got up to examine the objects more closely. The pitcher contained cold water, the plate a loaf of bread, a chunk of cheese, and a knife. "Bloody confident, aren't you?" she said aloud.

A glance showed her that the curtain was all the "door" this room had. God willing, she'd find her way out of this place. But not without fortifying herself for the quest. She washed, grimacing at her wrinkled, sweaty clothes, then ate and drank. She had fleeting doubts about the food, for wasn't eating anything in the realm of Faerie supposed to trap the victim forever? She decided, though, that the bread and cheese were commonplace country fare, doubtless stolen from a nearby farm. *What do elves eat, anyway?* Glancing around at the walls, she wondered what had happened to the jewels and rainbows. *They cast a glamour on me, I daresay. Isn't that what fairies are supposed to do?*

Well, they wouldn't get another chance. Bundling up in her shawl, she switched on the torch, clutched the bread knife, and stepped into the tunnel.

The clammy darkness seemed to grip her by the throat. She concentrated on the circle of light from the torch. Picking her way step by step over the smooth tunnel floor, she muttered reassurances to herself. The walls were *not* contracting around her. The light guiding her feet was real; all else was delusion born of her own fear.

The flaw in her plan struck her the first time the tunnel split into three. She did not know the way to the entrance. She had been in a trance when Tammas had carried her into the mound. She couldn't even hope to find the chamber where she'd met the child, for she'd been brought away from there unconscious.

Still, Judith didn't consider giving up. How far could these tunnels extend? If she walked long enough without doubling back on her path, she had to stumble upon the exit. Choosing at random, she took the right-most fork.

Several turns later, she began to lose confidence. The labyrinth showed no signs of coming to an end. She met neither of the elves and saw no rooms with opulent furnishings like the one she'd been taken to. Only a candle, now and then, burning in a wall sconce. Aside from that, she could almost believe she'd wandered below ground in some sort of brain fever and dreamed the rest. Soon she was breathing hard, her teeth chattering from the chill on her clammy skin. Fear rose like bile in her throat. Seized by panic, she began to run. Her own panting and the beat of her shoes against stone thundered in her ears.

She fell headlong on the floor, dropping the torch and the knife. She scrabbled for them in the undulating flame of a nearby candle. As she sat up, light in one hand and knife in the other, a curtain in the wall several yards away billowed and parted.

Tammas strode toward her.

Judith scrambled to her feet. When the light fell on the elf-lord's face, his eyes gleamed red. She brandished the knife, though a voice in the back of her mind told her the dull blade wouldn't kill a creature that could survive a bullet wound such as Liam had suffered. Surely the man was stronger than the child.

His burning eyes didn't flicker toward the weapon. Instead, he gazed steadily at her. As before, she felt lightheaded. A multicolored aura shimmered around the elf. Judith's fingers went slack. She hardly noticed when the knife slipped out of her grasp. When Tammas' cold fingers crept up her arms, a paradoxical rush of warmth swept over her.

"You can't attack us," he said in that clear, remote voice. "Don't waste your energy in the attempt. Liam needs you serene and whole."

She felt his arm around her waist. A sphere of light enfolded her. She thought she glimpsed fireflies dancing in alcoves in the rocky walls.

An instant later she found herself in the vaulted chamber with the wide bed. The boy Liam raised his arms to embrace her, and her head whirled with bright images whisked away before she could grasp them, like rose petals in a high wind.

Again Judith woke chilled and stiff. Her throat was sore, parched with thirst. After a drink and a hasty wash, she checked her cell. The torch and knife had been returned. She startled herself with a harsh laugh. Letting her keep the feeble weapon seemed a mockery; both she and the elves knew well that she couldn't harm them. In addition to her other supplies, she found oil for the lamp and a stack of folded clothes.

Simple cotton garments, she noticed. She wondered whether Tammas had stolen the clothes from some farm wife's bedroom or actually bought them. Judith washed more thoroughly, shivering, and dressed from the skin out. The skirt and bodice were a bit large for her but warmer than her own frock.

After another drink of water and a meal of the bread, sausage, and apples that had been left on the platter, she contemplated her prison. Her spirits drooped at the realization that no one would search for her. She had no living relatives; her few friends knew she often traveled for months at a time. At once she discarded the thought of another escape attempt. The terror of fleeing through the tunnels with no idea of her destination was still vivid. If she hoped to get out, she would have to persuade Tammas or Fiona to release her.

Oh, really? How?

To hold off the despair that threatened to swamp her, she picked up the sketchpad and pencil. Her drawing of the "elf-mound" faced her. Shaking her head, Judith flipped to a clean sheet of paper. Almost without conscious volition, her pencil raced over one page, then another. When she paused to flex her cramped fingers, she had produced a rough sketch of the child Liam lying in his silk-draped bed and a pale imitation of Tammas' and Fiona's chill beauty. The dazzling luxury of their chamber as she'd seen it utterly eluded her.

How much was real? Had everything but the boy's embrace been part of the glamour? And what did he need her for, anyway? In legend the faerie folk kidnapped nursing mothers, not spinsters, to feed their children.

Inaction and stale air made her drowsy. Some time later, a rustle in the shadows woke her from a light doze. When she caught her breath, she saw the boy, Liam, standing over her.

Barefoot, he wore a loose silk shirt over a pair of short trousers. He rested one hand on the wall, as if unsteady on his feet.

"What are you doing here?" said Judith. Slowly she stood up, her cramped legs trembling. "Should you be out of bed? You don't look well." *Absurd, I don't know how he ought to look!*

"My mother and Tammas are still asleep, and I wanted you." His voice would have graced any cathedral's boys' choir. He lowered himself to the heap of blankets that served as Judith's bed and sat cross-legged, staring at her.

Cautiously she sat near him, fascinated by the gleam of red at the centers of his silver eyes. "How did you find me?"

He looked mildly surprised at the question. "I felt you, of course. How could I miss you, when there are no others of your kind here? And I've touched you twice already."

"Touched? You mesmerized me, you and your--uncle." But no human practitioner could have controlled her mind so thoroughly. If this power wasn't magic, it was close enough. "What do you want?"

"I'm thirsty." He reached for her.

She flinched at the touch of his cold fingers on her wrist.

"Don't be afraid. I wouldn't hurt you."

The glow in his wide eyes drew her in. Submitting to the child's embrace, Judith lapsed into a delicious dizziness.

Some time later, she felt his cold lips leave her throat. Scanning his face, she gasped at what she saw.

His tongue flicked out to lick the blood from his lips. "Please don't be afraid. Your fear hurts me."

She sensed he was speaking of concrete physical pain. Numbly she rubbed her neck. She stared at the red stain on her fingertips.

Liam's cool fingers stroked her forehead. "The bleeding will stop presently."

Lines from Keats flashed into her mind: "I saw pale kings, and princes too, Pale warriors, death pale were they all... I saw their starved lips in the gloam..." She'd never understood "La Belle Dame Sans Merci" before, portraying the elven queen with horror as well as fascination. "You drink--"

"Why does that disturb you so much?"

In spite of the revulsion she tried to cling to, his feathery caress and mild voice soothed her.

"You eat the burned flesh of dead animals. The very thought sickens me!"

"That's different." Judith shivered.

Liam handed her the shawl, then poured her a mug of water, which she automatically drank. Trying to steady herself, she considered what a sensational story this experience would make--if she ever saw the outside world again.

"You're going to kill me."

A pained look passed over his face. "Certainly not. We hardly ever kill human beings, only animals. That is how I got wounded."

Judith remembered the local rumors about this place. "The cattle."

Liam bent his knees and wrapped his arms around them, so like a human boy that Judith wondered again if she were dreaming. "I wasn't allowed to go near human dwellings. I'm supposed to take wild animals, or livestock wandering on the moors. But I was curious. Mother and Tammas never let me get close enough for a good look at those people. You're the first day person I have ever spoken to."

"A farmer caught you on his property and shot you?"

Liam nodded. "I fled for home, and Tammas found me when I collapsed on the way. I was unconscious most of the time until he brought you. I've never tasted human blood before--I'm really too young, but the wound--"

His casual reference to his diet made Judith cringe against the wall. To deflect her thoughts from the subject, she said, "How old are you?"

"Only twelve. I should not have started for, perhaps, another four years. Tammas will be surprised that I could bespell you without his help." Liam smiled with a disarmingly childlike air of pride. Judith almost felt like patting him on the head in congratulation.

Watch out, that's part of their glamour! He's still a wild beast.

"Tammas is your mother's brother? Don't you have a father?"

Liam looked puzzled. "Of course. Didn't you? But I don't know who he was. Why should I?"

"My people would think it very odd not to know your father."

"Tammas has told me how your kind live, with both parents together all their lives. He says you can endure it because your lives are so short."

Judith almost laughed aloud at this cynical view of marriage. "And what about you? Your mother has to bring you up by herself?"

"She has my uncle's help, as you see. They are very close, because they are twins." He tilted his head as if listening. "Tammas has just awakened. It's sunset, and he is looking for me."

Forgetting her earlier horror of him, Judith grasped Liam's arm. "Listen, you have to help me get away. Tomorrow, when they're asleep, show me the way out."

"Oh, no, I cannot do that." He stroked her hand as if quieting a nervous kitten. "I need you. You brought me back from the void--I wouldn't have died, but I might have fallen into a living death and never awakened."

"All right," she whispered. "I'm glad I could help, but I can't stay--" She broke off, for now even her ears picked up approaching footsteps.

Tammas flung aside the curtain and glared at the two of them. "Liam, you should not be out of bed."

The boy stood up to face his uncle. "I am strong enough to walk, and I awoke hungry. I didn't have any trouble with her."

"So I see." Tammas' eyes glided over Judith. "You appear unharmed."

She clenched her fists at her sides, too indignant to be properly frightened. "Let me go!"

"That isn't possible. Liam needs human prey, and he is both too weak and too inexperienced to forage outside, even with our help. You will be well cared for."

"Until I waste away and die, I suppose?" When he gazed at her coolly without answering, she went on. "I refuse to thank you for the clothes. You probably stole them anyway."

"In this case, yes. But we do occasionally walk among your kind and make purchases with honest coin." He leaned against the stone wall with his arms folded, eyebrows arched in what might have been amusement.

"You're not really elves, are you?"

Tammas shrugged. "What's in a name, as your poet says. In this region, that is what the people call us, and we've found it advantageous to play that role. We are nocturnal, we cloud men's minds with our 'magic', and we live a very long time. Why not elves?" He turned to Liam. "Come along, you must rest."

From the threshold, Liam looked back at Judith. "I may come here again, mayn't I, Uncle? I don't need your help anymore, and I like talking to her."

After a moment's thought, Tammas gave a curt nod, then led the boy away. Judith flung herself down on the bedroll and gave way to hysterical sobs.

After a while, exhausted into calm, she admitted to herself that she couldn't pretend she was delirious or dreaming. She was the captive of blood-drinking faerie folk. With no malice whatever, as casually as Judith might milk a cow, the "lord" would keep her here as nourishment for Liam until she died. Her only hope was to work on the boy's nascent fondness for her.

Well, I won't die anytime soon, that's certain! I'll show the bloody beasts!

To that end, she needed to maintain her physical health as long as possible. She forced herself to eat the rest of the food on the platter. After that, she performed a series of setting-up exercises in the limited confines of the chamber. Determined to cling to mental health as well, she sat with her sketchpad and tried to ignore the darkness clustered around her.

Judith passed uncounted hours drawing, pacing her cell, reading books brought to her by Liam, and talking with the boy. Ample though monotonous food filled the plate at frequent intervals. Her discarded clothes vanished, to reappear clean and folded. She wondered whether Tammas or Fiona mesmerized some local housewife into doing the laundry and forgetting about it.

Soon after their first meeting, Liam brought her a leather-bound copy of *A Tale of Two Cities* and insisted they read aloud to each other. He knew nothing about human life and wanted to know everything. Judith struggled with the double burden of trying to explain the customs of a foreign country a hundred years in the past.

The child seemed fascinated by Judith's own past and questioned her endlessly about her home, family, and work. Amused by his naivete, she couldn't remain repulsed or frightened by him. She went into detail about the pleasures of the outside world and her sadness at missing them, in hopes of awakening his sympathy. If he were capable of that emotion--she couldn't tell whether his fondness for her was anything more than a spoiled child's attachment to a favorite toy.

"I'm so tired of staying down here," he complained on one occasion. "I miss the night. My mother and uncle say I'm not well enough to go out."

"I'd be glad to walk with you," said Judith, "just outside the mound for a few minutes."

Liam gave her a sly smile. "Yes, I know. So you could run away."

Judith suppressed a sigh. *He's ignorant but not stupid. I should have known.*

He nestled into her arms, as he often did. "I'm very glad you're here. Without you, I would be terribly bored. Besides, you taste good."

She couldn't suppress a wry smile at his outspokenness. Against her will, she'd actually grown to like this creature. *I suppose pet dogs like their masters, too. Doesn't mean I'd want to be a pet.*

"I can't stay forever, Liam. I don't belong here, I need the sun."

He listened with his usual air of bland incomprehension.

"Listen, once when I was little I found a half-grown baby bird under a tree in our back garden. My father splinted its broken wing, and I fed it by hand, day and night. After a couple of weeks, it was well enough to fly. I wanted to keep it for a pet. Can you guess what Father did?"

Liam gazed at her with his usual wide-eyed attention.

"He made me let the bird go. He said a wild thing could never be happy in a cage. Animals have to live the way nature intended. I threw a crying fit, but he wouldn't give in."

Liam mulled over the anecdote in silence for a minute. "I see. But this is different. The bird could not understand. You can understand why I need you here."

Judith shook her head in exasperation. "I'll become ill, and then what good will I be to you?"

"I won't allow that to happen." His fingers caressed her neck, sending shivers through her. "I wish you could *show* me what life in the day world is like. If you tasted my blood, you could--we could speak mind to mind. But Mother says it's too dangerous, especially at my age."

"Dangerous for you, you mean." Not likely that Fiona would waste a thought on Judith's welfare, except as it affected Liam. Repulsive as the thought of drinking blood was, Judith would almost welcome it to experience true telepathy.

"She thinks I depend too much on you already," said the boy. "She says that bond would place my life in your hands." His confiding embrace made it clear that he wasn't too worried about that risk. "She says I would become like an opium-eater craving the drug--whatever that means."

"If she's so concerned, she should let me go, and the problem would disappear."

Liam wrapped his arms around her neck. "I don't want you to go. And my mother says it is not safe to dispose of you until I'm completely recovered."

Dispose of me? Liam seemed oblivious to the implications. Judith, however, suspected that Fiona had meant something more final than turning her loose on the downs.

The boy didn't feed on Judith every time he visited, but he always hugged her, as if he drew strength from her body warmth. She disregarded the drained sensation she felt after his visits, for his touch gave her a languorous pleasure she blushed to contemplate. When he left her alone, she couldn't ignore the dampness, bare walls, and sour odor of her cell. Reading and sketching gradually lost the power to distract her from her monotonous existence. She couldn't tell day from night and quickly lost count of her sleep periods.

She felt at ease only when Liam came to her. His glamour, though nowhere near as powerful as his uncle's, softened the contours of the cell and veiled its walls in a shimmering glow. She was glad when he began to take his deathlike day-sleep in her chamber. His nearness, even in a trance so deep she couldn't tell whether he breathed, warded off loneliness and kept her fears remote and unreal.

The time came when he glided into her room with his eyes aglow. "Judith, they're taking me above at last. They say I may be well enough to hunt!"

She knew Tammas and Fiona had been bringing Liam rabbits and other small game all along, to supplement Judith's scant but frequent donations. She also knew how Liam had missed being allowed to chase his own prey.

He handed her an apple. "Here, eat this, it's fresh. Isn't this wonderful news?"

Aware that he was watching anxiously, Judith bit into the fruit. More and more often, Liam had to remind her to eat. "Yes, it's wonderful that you're getting stronger. I'm happy for you. Enjoy your--excursion."

Liam hurried off without further conversation. His excitement made Judith's nerves tingle, too. If only she could go outside with him. After he'd left, she wished she had thought of following him. But no, Tammas and Fiona would have sensed her presence instantly.

Judith began languidly combing her hair with the silver comb Liam had brought her some time ago. She didn't bother with the mirror; who cared how she looked?

Tears gathered in her eyes at the thought of being shut down here while Liam ran free. And soon he wouldn't need her anymore--

Judith sat up straight and dropped the comb. The thought shocked her awake like cold water in the face. As soon as the boy ceased to need her, the adults would "dispose" of her. Judith got to her feet. For a few seconds, a surge of dizziness forced her to lean on the wall. Her legs felt stiff from the dampness. She realized this weakness had plagued her for a long time; Liam's constant presence had kept her from noticing.

She sank to her knees and rummaged in her small pile of possessions for the hand mirror. In the lantern's glow she examined her pale, thin face. She saw violet half-circles beneath her eyes. Stretching out one hand, she checked her fingernails. They were blue-tinged. *Anemia.*

She had to escape. If Fiona didn't kill her, Judith knew she would die eventually anyway. With her health so impaired, it was a wonder she hadn't already developed pneumonia. *How long have I been down here? As long as a month?* Smiling bitterly, she picked up the knife they had never bothered to take from her. The "weapon" mocked her helplessness. Her inability to find her way out of the underground labyrinth remained the major obstacle to her escape.

Judith paced the cell, forcing warmth into her weakened limbs, until Liam returned.

He greeted her with a hard embrace. When his lips brushed her temple, she noticed they radiated heat instead of the usual chill. "If only you could have been with us! The moon is full, and--"

She gripped his shoulders. "Listen to me!" she whispered. "If you're well, your mother won't want me here anymore. She doesn't approve of my--influence--over you. She'll kill me."

Liam flinched, as if Judith's fear caused him pain. "She would not do that, after what you've given to me."

"Stop lying to yourself! She will. You have to guide me out, as soon as they're asleep."

Liam shook his head. "You excite yourself for nothing. I would never let them hurt you." He released her and reclined on his nest of cushions and blankets. "Now I want to rest. You promised to read me Mr. Dickens' *Christmas Carol.*"

Judith gave up the argument. Liam saw reality as he wanted to see it. *Don't we all?* she reminded herself. She tried to tame her tumultuous emotions as she picked up the book and read aloud: "Marley was dead, to begin with..."

Later Judith gnawed at futile escape plans while she watched Liam sleep. She knew she had to act before she drifted back into the nebulous dream state that had possessed her--how long? Several weeks, at least. She knew Tammas and Fiona spent each period from sunrise to sunset in a virtual coma, unlike Liam, who, since he was younger, needed less sleep. So during the day Judith could simply walk out, unhindered, if she knew the path. If only she could induce Liam to guide her. That prospect looked hopeless. The adults obviously thought so, or they wouldn't risk leaving Judith free to move about.

She wished she could pluck the facts from Liam's mind as easily as he sensed every nuance of her emotions. Something nibbled at the edges of her thoughts--something she ought to remember. Suddenly it came to her. *Maybe I can read his mind!* What had Liam said about sharing blood? If she tasted his blood, it would forge a bond between them. Their minds would lie open to each other.

But he wouldn't do that. His mother's prohibition had frightened him into abandoning the idea.

Why can't I just take what I need from him? Judith fingered the hilt of the knife. What she was contemplating made her queasy. She had to act quickly or lose her nerve. First she paced up and down the chamber a few times to loosen her muscles for the hike ahead. She breathed deeply to calm her racing heart. Then she knelt beside Liam and picked up one of his limp arms.

As she'd expected, the mere touch didn't wake him. She had become too familiar a presence. If she hadn't known better, his cold flesh would have made her think him dead. Not giving herself time to falter, she nicked his wrist with the point of the blade. A bead of blood appeared.

It's red, like mine. Not the ichor of the gods. How much would she have to consume? She swallowed against a wave of nausea. *Hurry up, get on with it.*

She lifted his wrist to her mouth and licked the drops oozing from the cut. No special taste, just a lukewarm fluid like her own blood.

Liam's eyes opened. Their silver glow drew her into a web of dancing lights. Her head whirled. A moment later, she was staring up at her own face. A rosy aura haloed her disheveled hair. *I'm seeing through his eyes!*

The chamber looked so bright, like summer twilight even though a single candle shed the only illumination. Yet the colors in her frock and the bedding were muted to pastels. The musty smell, channeled through Liam's senses, stung her. At the same time, she picked up the metallic scent of his blood and a hot, sweet fragrance that she realized must be her own flesh. It stirred hunger. Instead of feeling revulsion, she caught herself trembling with eagerness.

//No!// She didn't cry aloud. She knew, somehow, that she didn't need her voice to make him hear her.

She wrenched herself back into her own body.

Liam's face contorted with pain as if she had slapped him. //Judith, don't, that hurts. Why are you treating me this way?//

//Tell me the way out, now, or I'll gouge it out of your brain with my fingernails if I have to.//

//Don't leave me, please--would you give this up now that we have it?//

His pain twisted inside her, too, but she armored herself against it. She wouldn't throw away her only chance.

//Now, before your mother and uncle wake up.//

She felt his resistance, as if shoving against a door he was holding shut. She flung her loneliness and fear at the closed door. She felt Liam's resistance buckle under the strain. She battered him with the chill, the aches, the fatigue, the weakness she'd suffered from his feeding. A soundless cry from Liam shrieked inside her head.

//I'm dying down here, you God-forgotten little beast!//

//Stop--please--cruel--//

Judith turned her thoughts to her father's death and the desolation she'd felt after the funeral, finding herself alone in the world. When she poured out that anguish, Liam curled up inside himself, wailing.

//Let me out, or I'll blast you with pain you've never imagined!//

//Very well--stop--I never wanted to hurt you--//

She withdrew inside the boundaries of her own skull. For an instant the room spun. She groped in panic for support, afraid she had lost herself forever. Her senses came back into focus, though, allowing her to see normally again. Liam was holding her hands in a crushing grasp.

"I'm sorry I had to do that," she whispered. She realized she was shaking. "But I'll do it again if you don't keep your word."

"I will." He sank down on his pillow. "Now I understand why this bond is dangerous. To lose ourselves in a victim's--donor's--consciousness--" His voice was barely audible. He switched back to silent speech. //Go quickly. I shall guide you with my thoughts.//

Before she could weaken, she wrapped herself in her shawl and gathered up the electric torch and her sketchbook. Without the latter, she feared she would think this whole experience had been a delusion. At the last moment she ripped out one page, the best of her portraits of Liam. //A keepsake for you.//

//Step into the corridor and take the left-most fork,// Liam's whisper began in her mind.

Mechanically she followed the directions, using the light only where no candles shone on the walls. Her legs ached from the strain long before she reached the exit. After some immeasurable time, however, she did reach it.

Liam told her, //You have several hours until sunset. If you hurry to the nearest town, you'll be in no danger from my mother and Tammas.//

He directed her to climb a flight of crude stone stairs and pull a lever that moved a delicately balanced rock door. She stepped through the portal and found herself inside the barrow tomb.

//They use their mind-power to keep anyone from examining this mound too closely,// said Liam. //Now go, or I might try to lure you back. I could make you forget all that pain, make you happy with us--I know I could.//

A chill seized her at the memory of long hours during which she actually had been content as a pet confined in his lair. //Not the kind of happiness I want. Tell Tammas and Fiona not to worry, I won't talk about this place.// *Who would believe me?* //Goodbye, Liam.//

Afraid her own weakness would entice her back, with no help from him, she hastily stepped out of the barrow into the afternoon sun. It dazzled her eyes. She fell to her knees, gasping in the strange, brisk air of the open moor. Thinking of the Keats poem again, she murmured, "And I awoke and found me here--"

When her eyes adjusted, she scanned the deserted downs. The sun wasn't so bright after all, but overcast with clouds. The wind carried an unexpected chill. She had entered the mound on May Eve, and now the bleakness of autumn met her eyes.

"And I awoke and found me here," she recited aloud, "on the pale hill's side."

(Story originally published in *Kiss Of Death*, Darien, IL: Design Image Group, 1998)

Technical Adviser

The vampire waylaid Charlotte at 11 p.m. as she strolled to her car in the hotel parking lot. No Halloween-style special effects trailed in his wake, just a half-moon in a cloudless sky and the light breeze of a San Diego summer night. She thought she glimpsed a bat-winged shadow but blinked and dismissed it as illusion.

At the sight of the crimson gleam in his eyes, she thought, *Contact lenses.*

He stood a few yards away, blocking the driver's door of her Honda. He carried a book, which he held up as he said, "Miss Winters?"

By the weak glow from a lamppost a few lanes over, she identified it as her latest hardcover release, *Blood from a Stone. Oh, just a fan.*

"I'm sorry, the book signing ended an hour ago." Why did he accost her here instead of in the middle of a crowded convention? She fingered the zipper on her purse, thinking about the pepper spray can inside.

"I'm not here to get a book signed. I want to talk to you about the inaccuracies and injustice your work perpetuates."

Great! A crazy fan! "Why don't you write me a letter instead?"

"I have--several. You never answered." He took one stride toward her.

Of course not, I don't write back to the crazies. Charlotte reached into her purse and clutched the pepper spray. She glanced around the deserted parking lot. *Where are the fans when I need them?*

"You don't really want to do that." Suddenly he stood beside her, gripping her wrist.

She met his eyes and froze. *Yes, they glow--and I never saw him move.* "That didn't happen. You're some kind of hypnotist."

"Can't we skip this part?" He sounded wearily exasperated, rather than angry.

He wrapped his arms around her waist. She gulped. The ground dropped from under her. An instant later, she found herself hovering at second-story height above the parking lot. The wind sifted through her hair and brought tears to her eyes.

In a vertiginous swoop, he deposited her next to a white minivan about thirty feet away. With a wry smile, he handed her purse to her. "You aren't dreaming or hallucinating. This isn't hypnosis or special effects. Now that we have that out of the way, you're coming home with me so we can discuss your books."

Grabbing his sleeve to offset the tremor in her legs, Charlotte re-swallowed her stomach. "I don't think so!" She tugged at the chain of the silver Maltese cross she wore--a prop she always donned for public appearances--and thrust the ornament at him.

The man burst out laughing. "That's one of the inaccuracies. Get in." He opened the passenger door of the van. When she didn't move, he pried her fingers from the cross, stared into her eyes, and repeated, "Get in."

Her head swam. The next moment, she was seated in the van, buckling the seatbelt. *Neat trick! This would be a great way to escape those amateurs hounding me with the 500-page handwritten manuscripts.*

"What do you want with me?" Her voice, to her own disgust, sounded like a rabbit's whisper, if rabbits could whisper.

He flashed her a smile. "I feel your fear. Your heart's beating like thunder. I also feel that you want this." He patted her hands, fingers interlaced in her lap. His skin felt cool. "I give you my word, I won't hurt you."

Your word. Yeah, and do you want to sell me the Coronado Bridge, too? Yet his touch seemed to drain away her panic.

"Sure, in a way I want to hear what you've got to say. Just what I need, my own private interview--which I can't use."

"Yes, you can. To correct the errors in your portrayal of us." He revved up the engine and headed toward the highway.

"Somehow this isn't the kind of vehicle I would have expected."

"Did you think I would drive a hearse? The white paint reflects sunlight, the windows are tinted, and the car's roomy enough to sleep in, if necessary."

Glancing into the back of the van, she noted the dark curtains, open and tied back. "That's enough to protect you from the sun? Those drapes look pretty flimsy to me."

The vampire heaved a long sigh. "Miss Winters--Charlotte--sunshine doesn't make me burst into flame. It gives me a blinding headache--bad enough, since I can't take painkillers. That kind of Hollywood drivel is exactly why I want someone like you to clear the record."

"So why me?" She swept her hair back from her forehead. "I've never been on the best-seller list, much less had a movie with my name on it."

"You have more personal contact with your fans than most novelists," he said, "and you allow, even encourage, them to write about your characters in the so-called 'fanzines'. So you have many opportunities to disseminate truth in place of error. You see, I've researched you." He pulled onto Interstate 5, toward La Jolla.

"Gee, I'm flattered." She stole a glance at his square-jawed profile. *He doesn't look Transylvanish.* "You really want the world to know about you? How do the rest of your--people--feel about this?"

"I'm approaching you on my own. And I certainly don't want you to expose us in full daylight, so to speak. I simply want your fiction to become more realistic."

Realistic? She choked back a laugh. "Do I have this straight? You're going to tell me what to write?"

"Not at all--what a presumptuous notion," he said in a faintly shocked tone. "I'm only offering you my help."

Oh, Lord, he's worse than a fan! He's a wannabe collaborator! Another amateur with a manuscript. Even the one time she'd tried to collaborate with a fellow professional, a hopeless tangle had resulted. "Oh, all right, take me to your lair. I can't stop you anyway."

Shortly he turned off the freeway and slowed at the entrance to a townhouse complex surrounded by a high wrought-iron fence.

Charlotte watched him insert a card into the gate. "You live in a condo?"

"Security is good, and I don't have maintenance headaches. What did you expect, a castle?"

"Well, something a little more picturesque."

He eased the van into a carport, killed the engine, and walked around to open her door. "Like the sprawling Victorian mansion in your Count Morhaim trilogy? Can you begin to imagine the tax bite on those houses?"

Charlotte suppressed a groan. "Don't you have the accumulated wealth of centuries to fall back on?"

"I do have some money stashed away," he said, unlocking the front door, "but I work like everybody else."

"As what? History professor? Secret agent? Homicide detective on the night shift?" She caught a glimpse of a modestly landscaped courtyard, with the sparkle of a smallish swimming pool. "Obviously not an international financier."

He ushered her into a sunken living room paneled in blond wood. "An accountant." At her dismayed stare, he said, "It suits me very well. I can work at home, on my own schedule. Come to think of it, with the sales your work has enjoyed recently, you could probably use help with your investments. If you're interested in mutual funds--"

"Maybe another time." *I don't have to worry about having my blood drained; if I cross him, he'll bore me to death with spreadsheets!* She scanned the living room, decorated in Danish modern. "Let me guess--no coffin or native earth?"

With a derisive shake of his head, he asked, "What do you think I am, a mushroom? And why would I want to sleep in a box? I have a perfectly good master suite with a king-size bed and heavy curtains."

She sat on a low divan. "By the way, what's your name?"

"Call me Arthur. Arthur Kendall." He leaned over to shake her hand.

Charlotte sighed. The vampires in her romantic epics had names like Vladimir and Jean-Luc. They also had titles and estates. "Pleased to meet you, Arthur." His cool, firm grip sent shivers up her arm.

"Would you care for a glass of wine?"

She snatched her hand from his lingering clasp. "You never drink wine, of course."

"Sometimes I do. Right now, though, after the stress of waiting for you all evening, I need more substantial nourishment."

She leaped up and backed against a stereo speaker.

"Good grief, stop that! I'm not going to attack you. I have my own supplies."

He stalked through the dining nook to the kitchen. Charlotte followed, her breath coming in irregular gasps.

Arthur poured a glass of Chablis and thrust it into her hand. "Do you really think the scent of your flesh and the sound of your pulse will drive me into a feeding frenzy? Do *you* go into a frenzy at the sight of food?"

She dropped her eyes to the wine glass, embarrassed by her tactless response. "Well, if it's Godiva chocolate--"

While he opened the freezer, she inspected the room. *What does a vampire's kitchen look like?* Not much different from hers, only barer, without such amenities as a toaster and spice rack. Arthur placed a plastic bag of frozen blood in the microwave and switched on the "defrost" setting.

He warms his blood in a microwave? "You live on that?"

"For fresh meals, I depend mostly on raccoons and coyotes, the occasional horse or cow." He rotated the bag and reset the machine.

Charlotte watched him, getting her first good look. He had luxuriantly curly golden-red hair. In full light, she now saw his eyes as silver. Lean and well over six feet tall, he wore tight black jeans, black jogging shoes, and a *Star Trek* T-shirt. *I didn't expect a satin-lined opera cape, but couldn't he at least wear a silk shirt with lace cuffs?*

"What about--uh--human blood?"

"It's vital to our physical and mental health, but only in small quantities. We crave the emotional energy that flows with it." When his drink finished heating, he poured it into a pint mug with a Budweiser logo and led the way back to the living room.

"Drinking blood from strangers must be a lot more dangerous now than it was in the Middle Ages. Don't you worry about AIDS?"

"There's no reason why your new epidemic should affect us any more than the old, familiar ones did. We're immune to infection. We don't act as carriers, either, because we sense sickness, by body odor and the color of the subject's aura, and we avoid it. No predator wants diseased prey."

Sitting on the divan with her legs folded under her, she watched him sip the blood, glad the mug wasn't transparent.

Obviously noticing her expression of distaste, he said, "You really think this is worse than eating the charred flesh of dead animals? Come, now, the Masai drink blood as well as milk from their cattle. Marco Polo reported that the Mongols tapped the veins of their horses for nourishment. Victorian ladies and gentlemen visited slaughterhouses to imbibe blood for their health. And surely you've heard of blood sausage? Broaden your mind!"

"Okay, but don't expect me to try it!" She didn't even like raw oysters. "Are you going to show me your fangs?"

With another long-suffering sigh, he said, "I don't have fangs. I'm not a wolf or a rattlesnake. My incisors and canines are razor-edged."

"Then how come the inside of your mouth isn't bleeding all the time?"

"You don't bite yourself very often, do you? Neither do we."

She ogled his trim, youthful body, which looked no older than thirty. "How old are you, anyway?"

"I was born in 1256."

"So you died about seven hundred years ago?"

He emitted a sound remarkably like a snarl. "I've never died. I'm not a walking corpse or a fiend in human shape. We're another species, naturally evolved, like you. We just happen to stand higher on the food chain."

"Higher on the food chain! That's it?" *Where's the romance in that? My readers would never buy it.*

"We live much longer, obviously." With a smug grin, he added, "We have certain abilities beyond your grasp, and we're more intelligent."

Nettled, she said, "Yeah? If you're so superior, why haven't you taken over the world?"

When he'd stopped laughing, he said, "For one thing, we're a small minority compared to you. And why would we want to rule the world? Who'd want to go to all that trouble? You're doing all right so far, in your bumbling way, if you can manage not to poison it to death or blow it up."

"Next you'll tell me you can't even transform anyone into a vampire."

With a groan, he buried his face in his hands. "Hopeless! Think, Charlotte, do people bitten by mosquitos grow wings?"

She glared at him. "I'll bet you can't change into a bat, either."

"I weigh about a hundred and eighty pounds. The average bat weighs what?--four or five? Where would the extra mass go? Since matter can't be created or destroyed, it would transmute into energy. Instant tactical nuclear blast." He leaned back against the sofa, arms extended. "We do have, as one of our psychic gifts, the ability to make superficial alterations in our shape-- not size--and even temporarily sprout wings. We move very fast, and we can levitate, as you saw. But most of the shapeshifting legends are based on illusion--one thing we're very good at."

She watched him suspiciously. "You do hypnotize people, then."

"Yes, but I'm not tampering with your mind right now."

"How can I be sure?" *Waste of time to ask--I can't.*

"Trust me." He gave her a rakish smile. "Don't dismiss our brand of mesmerism until you've tried it. It's the main attribute that makes us sexually irresistible to your kind."

"Yeah, right." Did he sense the delectable quiver she felt when he looked at her? Probably. "So you father baby half-vampires?"

"No, not that kind of sex. It's almost impossible for us to interbreed with you. In fact, we seldom reproduce among ourselves. Long-lived creatures can't afford many offspring. Our sensual pleasures are focused--orally, as it were." This time his smile was definitely a leer.

Charlotte blushed hot. "Taking human blood really is like sex for you?"

"Yes, that's one thing you novelists got right." He raised his empty mug. "This has only taken the edge off my appetite. So if you're interested, for purposes of research--"

She inched farther into her corner. "Forget it, this is a business discussion. If you're so eager to set the record straight, why don't you write a book yourself?"

"We aren't creative by nature. Your species has that advantage over us. Besides, you have the contacts and the reputation to make sure the book gets read."

"It sounds as if you've been following my career for a while. Why did you decide to come to me now?"

His thick eyebrows drew together in a scowl. "It's that latest novel of yours, where Sir Oliver seeks a 'cure' for the 'curse' of his vampirism. I'm damn sick and tired of all those whining, self-pitying vampires who want to become human! What makes you think we envy clumsiness, sickness, infirmity, senility, and premature death? Who in his right mind would want to be human if he had a choice?"

She avoided his blazing eyes and murmured, "Well, we like it."

"We are not like you! I can't stand by any longer and watch you violate our integrity as a species. Would anyone publish a novel centered on a black man's desire to become white? Or an Asian's yearning to reshape her eyes? This 'curse' tripe is just as demeaning. We deserve as much respect as any other minority."

"Even if the public knew you existed--which you said you didn't want--you do have this reputation for ripping out people's throats."

"And that's another thing," he fumed, pacing. "Your villains. Your 'evil vampires' are worse than Iago, as far as 'motiveless malignity' is concerned. They all act like homicidal maniacs or rabid dogs. No vampire with a functioning brain would leave shredded, bloodless bodies around for the police to find. Not to mention--"

"All right, I get the point!" Maybe he did have some legitimate points, and certainly in her next novel, she wouldn't mind working on the villains and dropping the "cure" motif. But as for the rest of it--"Arthur, I can't screw around with generic conventions at will. My readers would never stand for it."

He glowered at her. "You value popularity and profit over truth?"

"I like profit. Profit is my friend. I have to eat, you know. As for truth, all fiction is an artificial construct made from selected elements of life."

He sat down again, close enough to touch her. She forced herself not to cringe. "Then you reject my demands."

"If you start 'demanding', darn right I do! So now what? You rip out my throat?"

"I would never do that without your permission. But I'm severely disappointed."

"I can't make a ninety-degree shift. It would never--uh--fly. But I'll tell you what I can do. We can collaborate. You supply the ideas, and I'll do the writing." *Collaborate? Did I really say that? Maybe he does have me hypnotized.* "My agent can peddle our books under a new pen name. Editors will know it's me, but the reading audience won't be upset by an abrupt switch."

He relaxed. "That sounds feasible."

"One condition. You're the technical adviser. You have editorial control over scientific and historical accuracy. *I* have the final say on plot and characterization. I know what works, and you said yourself you aren't creative. I won't stand for interference from an amateur, even one who's seven centuries old and has fangs."

"I do not have--"

"Take it easy, figure of speech."

He smiled, causing an annoying flutter in her diaphragm. "Very well, I have a condition, too. Let me control the investment of our mutual royalties."

"So we have a deal?"

He clasped her hand. "Deal." He gently kissed her fingertips. The flicker of his tongue made her pulse race. "Would you consider sealing the bargain with a drink, after all?"

Damn, he can probably hear my heartbeat; I can't hide anything from him. "Maybe, for purposes of research."

(Story originally published in *Night To Dawn 1*, Winter 2002)

Scavenger Hunt

ownstairs, Professor Gregory Lawrence's other guests began to drift toward the front door. Upstairs, Diane hid in a spare bedroom, fishing a flashlight out of her purse. Her medieval literature professor's voice, although one floor down, reverberated along her nerves. A shiver trickled down the back of her neck. Listening to him read from Malory's *Morte d'Arthur* an hour earlier, she'd reflected that he ought to be acting, not teaching night classes at a community college. His rich, faintly English-accented baritone belonged on a stage.

Diane shook off the inappropriate reverie and suppressed a sneeze from the dust in the unswept corner where she huddled. She had to reach her goal and get away without the professor catching her. It would be too humiliating to explain why she wanted to rummage through his dresser drawers.

Feeling as if she'd embarked on a Mad Hatter's scavenger hunt, she switched on the flashlight and tiptoed to the door. This sprawling late-Victorian house had a maze of rooms on the second floor. She hoped it wouldn't take too long to find the master bedroom. Already she ran short of time, for she hadn't expected most of the other students to leave the end-of-term party this soon. Tiptoeing and barely breathing, Diane prayed that her host had accepted her earlier fake departure as a real one--and that he would linger downstairs for a while.

With her ear to the closed door, she didn't hear anyone in the hall. A babble of voices still floated up from the living room and foyer. She worked her way down the hall, investigating each door. Most stood open and concealed no secrets. Sparsely furnished guest rooms, spaces empty except for stacks of boxes, a roomful of bookshelves to hold the overflow from downstairs, and a home office disappointed her.

Would she have to head up to the third level to find the professor's bedroom?

Briefly her mind veered into irrelevant speculation about that forbidden chamber. Did he cover his bed with satin sheets or utilitarian white cotton? Did he sleep in silk pajamas, bikini briefs, or nothing at all? Though she'd seen him only in sedate gray slacks and autumn-toned turtlenecks or sport shirts, his lean frame would probably look good in any one of those imagined sleeping costumes. That last thought made a hot blush suffuse her face.

Diane shook her head, annoyed with herself for fantasizing about a man whom she'd certainly never want to face again after this escapade. Only the trivial nature of her anticipated theft nerved her to go through with it.

She arrived at the last door on the second story. This one was shut. Hoping she'd found her goal, and praying that the hinges didn't squeak, she eased it open.

She slipped inside and pulled the door shut behind her. Underneath the dust that tickled her nose, she caught a faintly metallic scent. Her flashlight swept around the room. Another small bedroom, but this one had an occupant.

On the twin bed beneath the heavily curtained window lay a dark-haired boy, asleep. Stifling a gasp, Diane stared at him. Asleep or unconscious? He didn't react to the light shining on his face. With his milk-pale skin and almost emaciated thinness, she thought he must be sick. She couldn't decide whether he was an unusually tall twelve-year-old, an undergrown eighteen-year-old, or somewhere in between.

Abruptly she realized her unpardonable intrusion. She ought to be ashamed of herself, sneaking up on a sick boy. In fact, she felt ashamed of the whole crazy project. But if she couldn't hang onto her dream any other way-- *So find the stuff and get out of here!* she admonished herself.

As she groped behind her for the doorknob, she became aware that the farewell chatter downstairs had stopped. In the silence, she heard the door opening and felt a draft from the hall. Before she could turn around, a hand closed on her shoulder.

She jumped, swallowed a screech, and dropped the flashlight. Professor Lawrence caught it, then turned her to face him. For a second she thought she saw glints of red in his eyes. *Illusion--sudden change in the light, that's all.*

"Ms. Ferber, imagine meeting you here. After you so pointedly announced that you had to leave, too." His low voice began as a purr and segued into a growl. Returning the flashlight and drawing her into the hall, he closed the door.

He loomed over her, making her painfully aware of her below-average height. His hands now rested on her shoulders, with his thumbs tracing circles on the bare skin where her collarbone joined her neck. Her pulse hammered with nervousness and some other emotion she preferred to ignore. Thank goodness he couldn't hear her heartbeat. It was bad enough that he could see the patches of red on her heated face and probably feel her trembling.

"I'm really sorry, Professor--I'll go now--"

"Not until we've had a little talk, Ms. Ferber--Diane." Now he sounded more amused than angry. His dark, bushy eyebrows, almost joined above his nose, had a satanic slant. "And you may as well call me Greg." He guided her away from the door to lean with her back against the wall. His fingers crept up her neck to cup her head. Their gentle massage calmed her racing pulse.

In the back of her mind she wondered why she let him touch her this way without protest, but she enjoyed the sensation too much to pursue the thought. Though she felt a fleeting desire to run her own fingers through his thick, black hair, she didn't have the energy to follow the impulse. She contented herself with gazing up into his violet-gray eyes. Her muscles turned to jelly, allowing the flashlight to drop onto the carpet.

"Tell me, Diane," he whispered, "why are you searching my house?"

She felt lightheaded, almost floating. "I'm looking for your bedroom," she murmured.

"Indeed? Why?"

Faintly surprised to hear the words coming out of her mouth, she told the truth. "To get a pair of socks."

His voice hardened, no longer amused. "Why the devil would you want my socks?"

"I don't want them. My landlord does."

"Who is your landlord?"

"Ronald Horton." She gave a dreamy sigh, wishing the professor--Greg-- would stop asking questions and keep caressing the back of her neck. Or even kiss her. She swayed toward him, lips parted.

Instead, his fingers stilled. "Horton? Interesting. This man sent you to steal a pair of socks?"

"Actually, he just needs a left sock, but since left and right look the same, he told me to get a pair."

Greg's hands moved back to her shoulders, tightened briefly, then relaxed. "I see. You didn't simply ask me for them, why?"

"And look like a total idiot?"

"More of one than you look creeping around my house in the dark?"

The mockery in his voice reduced her to silence. Speaking up in class was one thing; embarrassing herself in front of a man she'd daydreamed about for months was something else!

"Diane, you live alone, don't you? Above your bookshop?"

She nodded, heavy-lidded with pleasure as he renewed his caress. Again she glimpsed a crimson gleam in his eyes, but the anomaly no longer disturbed her.

"Do you have any family nearby?"

She shook her head.

"Does anyone other than Mr. Horton know you're here right now?"

"No."

"Excellent." He smiled. "As soon as I noticed you'd stayed behind, I suspected you might be just what I need."

"For what?" Anticipation rippled along her nerves.

Slipping an arm around her waist, he led her into the bedroom they'd just vacated. "Don't be afraid," he whispered, his lips grazing her hair. He guided her to the bed, only a shadowy outline in the dark. Diane allowed him to seat her on the edge of the mattress. She heard the springs creak as Greg leaned over and murmured, "Daniel--wake up, Daniel."

The boy under the sheet stirred. A pair of glowing eyes appeared on the pillow. Still floating in the warm fog of the professor's touch, Diane registered this oddity without a trace of surprise or alarm.

"Now," Greg breathed, "give me your hand, my dear."

She would have given him her whole body if he'd asked. When he clasped her hand and guided it to the pillow, she noticed the coolness of his skin. The boy's lips, though, felt downright icy. By contrast, the heat of his tongue on the inside of her wrist startled her.

What am I doing here? She blinked, trying to force the dim room into focus.

"Don't worry," Greg whispered. His breath sent shivers down the back of her neck. Again a warm, fragrant mist clouded her brain. A second later, she couldn't recall what had bothered her.

She felt a momentary sting on her wrist, followed by a hot rush that flowed up her arm and suffused her body. She relaxed in Greg's arms and spiraled down to oblivion.

Relax, don't worry, rest, everything is perfectly all right. The voice whispered in Diane's head.

It's not all right, another voice retorted. *I still have to find--*What did she need to find? She couldn't remember.

Fighting against the tidal force that sucked her toward sleep, she opened her eyes.

She lay on a double bed in a small room, only about ten by ten. The air smelled dusty. By the sunlight filtering through the age-yellowed curtains, she saw a dresser and nightstand of dark wood. Two closed doors, one doubtlessly leading to a closet, completed the view. With sluggish effort she lifted her arms to trigger the backlight on her watch. Late afternoon, almost 4:30.

What was she doing here, wherever here was? Didn't she have work to do somewhere?

No, she'd closed the bookstore for a week of inventory. The thought of the store reminded her of Mr. Horton and the socks.

I'm in Professor Lawrence's house! Now she remembered the previous night, up to the moment the professor--Greg--had taken her into the room where the boy lay unconscious. After that, the details became fuzzy.

She remembered a sting on her wrist. Raising her left arm again, she squinted at a small incision. It didn't hurt.

Nothing to worry about, the alien voice murmured again. *You're content here. You can't leave the house. You don't even want to go downstairs.*

No, she didn't want to go downstairs. Nothing of interest there. She felt herself drifting into a warm haze.

Stop that! While she didn't have any particular interest in going downstairs, she couldn't lie here and fall asleep again. She needed those socks.

She put on her shoes, which she found beside the bed, and staggered across the room. Her head spinning, she leaned on the door for a moment before opening it. She groped her way to the bathroom. After splashing water on her face, she felt almost awake. She smoothed her curly, blonde hair, glad she kept it short enough that it hadn't become hopelessly tangled.

Last night she'd discovered that Greg didn't sleep on the second floor. Therefore, she had to explore the third. Listening at the foot of the stairs, she didn't hear any movement. Maybe she'd lucked out, and he wasn't home.

At the top of the steps she saw another hallway lined with doors, only one of them closed. Now that her eyes had adjusted to the gloomy interior, she stalked confidently to the shut door and pressed her ear to it. No sounds. With a sense of déjà vu, she turned the knob and crept inside.

It took her only a few seconds to confirm that she had indeed found the master bedroom. The presence of her sleeping host--or captor--proved it.

She froze, her eyes snared by the motionless body on the bed. Although dark drapes wrapped the chamber in artificial twilight, she could tell that the part not covered by the sheet--from the waist up--was bare. Diane caught herself tiptoeing in that direction.

What am I doing? Better get out of here now!

Too late. One second, Greg lay apparently dead to the world. The next instant, he'd flashed to her side. His hand grasped her arm.

She let out a squeak of alarm. Again her head reeled. When it steadied, she risked a glance downward. He wore a pair of satin running shorts. She didn't know whether the discovery left her relieved or disappointed.

The painful grip of Greg's chill fingers relaxed, but not enough for Diane to wiggle loose. "You are the most exasperating creature," he said. The half-smile that accompanied the remark didn't go far toward soothing the flutter in her stomach. His free hand brushed her hair back from her forehead and skimmed down her jawline to her throat. "Didn't I tell you to stay put?"

She breathed an almost soundless "No."

"Hmm." His fingers wandered from her throat to the back of her neck. "That's true, I simply ordered you not to go downstairs. What are you doing in my bedroom?"

"Socks," she whispered.

"Got a one-track mind, haven't you? Return to the room where you woke up and wait there. We have to discuss this."

Before she realized she had moved, she found herself in the hall with the door shut. Mechanically she obeyed Greg's last command and groped her way back from where she'd come. She ran a comb from her purse through her hair, then tried to tidy her rumpled blouse. The slacks, at least, were wrinkle-proof.

Why do I care how I look to him? And why am I still here? I should run like a rabbit. Admitting to herself that she cared too much what the professor thought of her, she knew that infatuation wasn't the main reason she didn't try to escape. He'd done something to her mind.

Minutes later, he walked in, strode to the bed, and sat beside her. He'd slipped on a navy blue T-shirt and a pair of tennis shoes. "I've watched you in class. You seemed to enjoy the course more than the other students. They treated it like a chore, just another three-credit elective."

"Probably because I took it for fun, not credits," Diane said. "I already have a degree, in business. Since my store specializes in used and rare fantasy and SF, I thought medieval lit would help me understand the field better. *Beowulf* has a monster and a dragon--the first English epic was a horror story. And think how many fantasy novels have been based on Arthurian legend."

"I don't usually read that kind of fiction. Perhaps I should." Was he genuinely interested or humoring her? He went on, "So Horton owns the building your shop occupies."

"I live there, too. It was about the only place I could afford where zoning laws allow me to live above the store. Mr. Horton owns most of the block."

"What do you know about him?"

"Well, he isn't in very good health. Has a chronic heart condition. And he's into the occult. Runs a New-Agey kind of shop, sells crystals, pyramids, herbal concoctions. He even has a coven, if that's what you'd call it, that meets there every week." Thinking of Horton made a chill seep through her veins. "He creeps me out. Sure, I like to read the fiction, but he really believes that stuff."

"Stuff?"

"The supernatural. It's nice to have him practically next door when the plumbing clogs up, but I wish he wouldn't hang around so much the rest of the time. Even if I feel sorry for him being sick, that doesn't mean I *like* the man."

"Then why are you stealing socks for him? Why didn't you tell him to go to the devil?" Greg asked the question in a flat tone, with no indication of anger.

Diane clutched her head, which began to ache as the warm, floating sensation faded. "I spent most of my capital--an inheritance from a great-aunt-

-building up my stock. Even with a sideline in mystery and romance paperbacks, I'm having trouble keeping up with expenses. I'm two months behind on rent."

"There's no one to help you? Parents, perhaps?"

"No way will I ask them for money." She punctuated the rejection with a vigorous shake of her head. "They wanted me to invest the inheritance in mutual funds and use my business degree for a nice, secure office job. They didn't exactly order me never to darken their door again, but things are--tense. I'm not about to go crawling back."

"So Horton offered to forgive the debt?"

She nodded. "He said he'd let the two months' rent go and give me an extra month free, too. All I had to do was snag a pair of your socks. It sounded so silly and harmless."

"Why did he choose you for this burglary?"

"He must've asked around about you. He found out you always throw these end-of-term parties for your students. So he knew I'd be in your house."

"Of course." Greg looked more thoughtful than outraged now. "Did he mention what he wanted the socks for?"

"No, but with his occult obsession, I could guess. Some kind of magical rite, I'm sure, like using a lock of hair in a voodoo doll. But I don't believe in that stuff, so I figured, why not. Even if magic really worked, I think Mr. Horton would have trouble killing a fly with a swatter, much less a man with a spell." Under the professor's steady gaze, she felt like crawling into the closet and curling up in a ball. "I'm sorry I trespassed on your privacy. I'll go now."

"Not so fast." He clasped her hand and traced circles on her palm with his thumb. Shivers ran up her arm. She felt the pulse in her neck throb. "Last night I said I needed you, and that hasn't changed. Daniel needs you."

She'd almost forgotten about the unconscious boy. "Needs--? Why?"

"Don't worry about that." Greg's voice dropped to a hypnotic murmur.

Hypnotic! He'd hypnotized her last night, and he was doing it again. "I'm not listening to you," she muttered. Speaking took as much effort as slogging through quicksand. "You put me in some kind of trance. Stop it."

"Very well," he said in a normal tone. "Mesmerized or not, you can't leave until I allow it. Come along. Daniel should be waking."

Walking down the hall hand in hand with her "host", Diane still felt eerily calm. Last night's hypnotic trance must have left a residual "don't worry" effect. "Who is he?"

"My sister's son. I'm responsible for him this week, and a hell of a job I've done. Horton injected him with a powerful sedative and drained a pint of his blood."

"Good grief, why?"

"The heart trouble you mentioned suggests a reason. I think Horton drank my nephew's blood in the hope that it might cure him."

"What?" Diane snapped awake from her pleasant daze and stared at the professor. "Where would he get that idea?"

"Probably because he thinks Daniel and I are vampires. Some Eastern European Gypsies believe one can trap a vampire by stealing its left sock."

"Vampires!" She came to an abrupt halt and stared up at him.

"Since the young one's blood didn't effect an instant cure," said Greg, "Horton must have concocted a plan to get control over a mature vampire-- me--and use my blood. Daniel managed to make it home before he lost consciousness, and Horton must have followed him and seen me."

"But why would he possibly think--" Her chest tightened. The pulse hammered in her temples. Remembering the glow of crimson eyes she thought she'd imagined, she felt the scratch on her wrist tingle.

Greg's eyes roamed up and down her body, at last settling on her face. "You're an intelligent young woman and obviously not afraid to believe your own senses, even if what they're showing you looks insane."

"You really are--something--not human." How else could he have hypnotized her with a mere glance and a caress?

"Shall I erase all this from your memory?" He drew her toward the closed door of the boy's room. "Let's discuss that later. You won't panic and disturb Daniel, will you?"

Aware of the professor's strength, she didn't fight him. Inside the bedroom, she gazed down at the unconscious boy, ivory-skinned and frail. "You fed him my blood last night," she whispered, "and you want to do it again."

"Only a modest amount. We need quality, not quantity, from our human donors. Pharmaceuticals often have unpredictable effects on our kind. I've already tried animal blood and my frozen blood bank stock to counteract the damage from Horton's drug. It didn't help. We need the vital fluids of someone like you."

"If you and your nephew are--aren't human, how did he get caught?"

"He's young and inexperienced." Greg smoothed a lock of hair off the boy's forehead. "He just recently began feeding from human donors. Horton stumbled across him in the act, lay in wait for him the next night, and disabled him with a spray bottle of garlic juice."

"Garlic, like in the movies?" That sounded almost as weird as a left sock.

"One of the legendary elements that's based on truth. When Daniel was helpless with nausea from the allergic reaction, Horton injected him and extracted the blood. The combination of the sedative and blood loss left him like this. I was hoping to find a donor at last night's party--and you fell into my hands. When I heard your footsteps on the second floor, I knew I didn't need to detain anyone else." He stroked Daniel's forehead again. "Wake up."

The boy's eyes slowly opened. Witnessing the red gleam in their centers, Diane believed everything the professor had said.

"Come closer," Greg murmured. He clasped her wrist and guided it to Daniel's parted lips. "Don't be afraid. Think of it as a simple donation." Massaging her back in expanded circles, he sent waves of heat surging through her body.

Donation? So do I get juice and cookies? Ripples of pleasure radiated from the point where he touched her. *Never mind, this is better than cookies.* She hardly noticed the boy's teeth pierce her skin. Far from painful, the drawing of her blood made her feel as if champagne bubbled in her veins.

Finally, lightheaded, she leaned back against Greg's chest, with his arms wrapped around her. Daniel's heavy-lidded gaze captured her eyes. In the dim light she saw him mouth the words, "Thank you," before he sank into apparent sleep. He looked so helpless that she couldn't fear him.

Her head began to clear when Greg guided her from the room. "Did you hypnotize me again?"

"No, what you felt was a normal side effect of nourishing one of us. Doesn't it make good evolutionary sense for a predator to lull the prey into enjoying the experience and coming back for more?"

"I don't know. I never heard of a mouse who liked being eaten by a cat."

Greg laughed softly. "Diane, I think I won't alter your memory, after all. I have a deal to offer you." He led her into his study, where he turned on the desk lamp and waved her to a leather-upholstered chair, while he sat behind the desk. "I'll give you a pair of socks for your slightly deranged landlord."

She blinked at him. "Oh? What about the Gypsy curse or whatever? Won't Mr. Horton have control over you?"

With a more robust laugh that made her stomach flutter, he said, "That's pure superstition, like at least half the nonsense people believe about us. We're not the walking dead, and those traditional magic tricks don't work. We're simply another species. An endangered one, at that, a persecuted minority."

"Hmph! A persecuted minority that bites!" He hadn't really hurt her, though, Diane reflected. So far, he hadn't even threatened her, but appeared to be giving her a choice. "You said a 'deal'--what do you want in exchange?"

"One more dose of your young, healthy blood. Promise to come back tomorrow night, and I'll let you go unhindered."

"How do you know I'll keep my word?"

"You kept your harebrained bargain with Horton."

She felt herself blushing. "Well, I thought he might be watching me, so if I tried to trick him with a pair I'd bought, he'd find out."

"More important," said Greg, "I'll know your promise is sincere, because we can read emotions. You can't lie to me."

Heat spread from her face to shoulders and bosom in a searing rush. So he must have sensed every vagrant feeling that had flitted through her mind while she'd sat in class weaving X-rated scenarios with him in the starring role.

"So you'd better go now." The professor stood up. "The sooner you give Horton what he wants, the less likely he'll wonder what delayed you."

Still dizzy from the racing of her heart, Diane got to her feet, clutching the back of the chair. "Right--he's probably been watching for me most of the day."

Minutes later, she stood in the foyer with her purse in one hand and a rolled-up pair of black socks in the other. Greg leaned over to kiss her cheek. The swift brush of his lips made her quiver inside the way no passionate kiss from an ordinary man ever had.

"May I hope that tomorrow night won't be your last visit? I admire your determination. I'd like to know you better." The way his voice deepened and lingered on the word "know" accelerated her pulse all over again.

She escaped to her car and drove home in the twilight, with both hands tightly gripping the wheel to stop their shaking. Only when unlocking the door to her apartment above the shop did she think to wonder whether Greg's invitation was sincere or merely a ploy to sweeten his request for another "dose" of her blood.

The next evening at sunset, she pulled into Greg's driveway. In her purse she had Mr. Horton's signed receipt for three months of rent. Now that she didn't have to worry about making up the shortfall and had an extra month's breathing room besides, she felt sure she could stay caught up. She wouldn't lose the store. That certainty was well worth a few minutes of wheezing gratitude from her landlord, even with his breath reeking of the cigarettes that doubtlessly contributed to his cardiac trouble.

Well, that and one more blood-donating session.

Pounding the knocker on the front door, she wondered how much of her memory from the previous night could be accurate. Professor Greg Lawrence, a vampire? Or some kind of alien predator behind the vampire legends? Could his hypnotic talent have implanted that belief to cover up something even more bizarre?

When he opened the door and let her in, though, all her doubts drained away. Gathering her into his arms, he skimmed his lips over the top of her head, his breath stirring her hair. "I knew you were brave and honorable as well as determined. Thank you for returning."

"I had to, didn't I?" Her breath caught in her throat. She forced a tremulous laugh. "Or else you'd track me down."

"I might, but never to harm you." His hands wandered over her back, one coming to rest at the nape of her neck, where the cool touch sent ripples down her spine.

She struggled to keep her thoughts from tangling in the web of his allure. "How's Daniel?"

"Improving--but he can wait a moment or two." Greg nibbled at her earlobe, then the hollow of her throat. With a gasp, she tightened her arms around him, afraid she might collapse. His mouth explored the corners of hers. She parted her lips, eager for the tantalizing flicker of his tongue to meet hers.

The door behind her banged against the wall.

She whirled halfway around, with Greg's hands still loosely clasping her arms. Horton stood on the threshold. Looking perfectly ordinary in faded jeans and a wrinkled blue shirt, with a few days' beard stubble on his thin, middle-aged face, he brandished a rosary in one hand and what looked like a spear in the other.

"Let her go, spawn of the devil!" he growled, shaking the rosary at Greg.

Diane's stomach clenched with fear. "No, Mr. Horton, you don't understand--"

Greg maneuvered her out of the way and took a long stride toward the intruder. "You don't want to do this," he said quietly. "Believe me, you don't."

Horton jabbed the spear in Greg's direction but seemed hesitant to take the risk of attacking. "Don't try to use your powers on me, vampire."

"Mr. Horton, what are you doing here?" said Diane. "You got what you wanted."

"I shouldn't have made you risk your life like that," he said in his hoarse grumble. "My spell didn't work anyway. So I decided to take direct action. Now, you let her leave, vampire. I'm the one who's after you."

"What are you talking about?" Diane had little hope she could deflect Horton from his obsession, but she had to try. "There's no such thing as a vampire. You're harassing Professor Lawrence for nothing."

The man's breathing grew more labored. "You don't know about these things the way I do. I recognize the signs--he's a minion of evil--"

She glanced between the two men, Horton gripping his weapon like a primitive hunter, Greg tensed like a tiger about to spring. She knew that if Horton attacked, he would have no chance against a predator in human shape.

Suddenly Greg's comment about superstitions leaped into her mind. "That's ridiculous, and I'll prove it!" She dashed to Horton and snatched the rosary from him.

Her eyes met Greg's. He stood unflinching while she raised her arm to press the crucifix on the end of the rosary against his forehead.

She darted a glance at Horton. "You see? He's just an ordinary man."

Picking up the cue, Greg took the rosary from her and curled his fingers around the cross. "See? Doesn't hurt a bit. I suggest you revise your theory, Mr. Horton."

The intruder's arm went limp, letting the spear dangle from his fingertips. "But that boy--I saw what he did--"

"Your eyes can deceive you. Don't believe everything you think you see." Greg gently pushed Diane aside and stepped forward to glower down at Horton. He tucked the rosary in the man's shirt pocket. "In fact, you shouldn't remember everything you think you see." He placed his hands on either side of Horton's head, fingers drawing circles on the temples. "Forget all about my nephew. You never saw him. You never saw this house, much less entered it." Horton's face went slack, making him look older and sicker than normal. "You don't believe in vampires. And you would never think of killing anyone, would you?"

Horton slowly shook his head.

"Go home and forget about me. Forget about this vampire nonsense. It was all a mistake." A weary nod was the only reply. "Oh, and by the way, quit smoking. You won't miss it a bit."

Spinning the man around, Greg hustled him onto the porch and locked the door behind him.

"That was a good thought," Diane said, "making him quit."

"That'll do more for the idiot's heart than vampire blood would. And I never could stand the odor of cigarettes anyway." He glided to Diane and embraced her.

She snuggled against him, standing on tiptoe to wrap her arms around his neck. "For a minute I was afraid he'd really try to murder you."

"I'm glad of your concern, but he wouldn't have succeeded," said Greg with a sardonic smile.

"Yeah, that was my other worry, that you'd kill him."

Greg stared down at her in mock indignation. "What, ruin my perfectly comfortable life here and have to start over somewhere less pleasant?" He nuzzled her neck. "I have another reason for wanting to stay now."

The familiar lightheaded sensation swept over her. "Good, because I want you to stay. I want to know you better, too."

"One potential problem," he said. "It's pushing the limits of my control over Horton to have you in his sight constantly, day in and day out, reminding him of this episode. Do you think it's absolutely necessary to live above your shop?"

She leaned back to gaze into his eyes, puzzled. "Like I told you, it's the only place I can afford to live."

"On the contrary, you might want to expand your business to the living quarters. You could double or triple your stock, with a cash gift--or a loan, if your pride insists we call it that."

She still didn't get the gist of his suggestion. "I don't understand. Where am I supposed to live?"

He gave her a feral smile. "Here, of course," he said before he kissed her again.

(Story originally published in *Night To Dawn 1*, Winter 2002)

Incunabula

A knock at the door woke Denise from her doze on the lumpy couch. She glanced at the black and white flicker of the TV screen, then at the digits on her watch. After eleven.

Grumbling. she dropped the book from her lap, tugged her forest-green William and Mary sweat shirt over the waistband of her jeans, and plodded to the door. Her hand on the knob, she blinked further awake and hesitated. Jack the Ripper? On the wooded verge of a restored Colonial town inhabited half by college students and half by tourists?

She raked her fingers through her unfashionably long, straight, chocolate-brown hair and opened the door.

Her rented house stood at the end of a narrow lane with no street light except at the corner where it met the county road. To see who waited on the sagging wooden porch, Denise had to switch on the overhead lamp. She confronted a face that made her wonder if she were still dreaming. *Wuthering Heights* had teleported her into the *Twilight Zone* rerun she'd been watching, for here was Heathcliff in the flesh.

Actually, there was nothing brooding or menacing about her old friend Nigel Jamison. His curling black hair and smoky gray eyes, however, befitted a hero of Victorian romance. Leaning against the doorjamb, arms folded, he looked down at her with a casual smile of greeting more suited to high noon than the middle of the night. His charcoal-gray slacks and alligator-adorned navy shirt made her feel like hiding her tousled self in a closet.

"Glad I caught you at home, Denise."

His voice, after almost two years, still resonated through all the cavities of her body. Damn. What right had he to show up at this unearthly hour, after his infrequent one-page letters, and still have such a devastating effect on her?

"Nigel, is it you or a ghostly visitation? And if not the latter, why couldn't you pick a more civilized time?"

"It's not exactly a short drive from Charlottesville to here," he said. "And you know I don't like to drive before dark, which comes fairly late in the middle of June." Nigel, in addition to numerous other allergies, suffered from photosensitivity.

"Then you could've at least phoned first."

"I was afraid you might refuse to let me visit," he said with the slow smile that had always torn her better judgment to shreds. "I figured you'd be less likely to slam the door on me in person." Inhaling deeply of the humid air, he added, "It really is a beautiful night, but I'd hoped you would let me in."

"Oh, all right," she sighed. "I hate to admit it, but I'm glad to see you."

This meeting was their first since his graduation from William and Mary, in the class ahead of Denise's. While he'd entered the University of Virginia's Ph.D. program in psychology, she had stayed in Williamsburg to pursue an M.A. in English, a degree that she sometimes thought was fleeing from her at supersonic speed.

She felt no embarrassment about admitting Nigel to her four-room furnished house. He knew what a graduate student's stipend would bear, though money had never posed a problem for him. He stretched out on the faded floral-print couch, arms flung wide along the back cushions, claiming, in typical masculine style, more than his share of space.

Switching off the TV, Denise said, "Now that you're here, can I get you a drink?"

"Milk."

She might have guessed; he seldom drank anything else. After bringing him a glass, she poised expectantly on the edge of the rocking chair. Let Nigel make the next move, blast him.

After a leisurely survey of her Arthur Rackham fairy tale prints on the wall, he said, "Actually, I drove down here to ask you a favor."

A-ha! she mentally pounced.

"A pretty big one," he said, uncharacteristically diffident. "Denise--am I wrong to think you care about me?"

You're not wrong, damn you, she silently grumbled. *You shameless manipulator!* If he'd asked, two years before, she would probably have married him. Her face tingled with heat. Her only consolation through those years when they'd maintained an anomalous "best friends" relationship had been his total lack of interest in other women. Or men, for that matter.

When his silence stretched beyond a normal conversational pause, she said, "Well, what if I do? What's the favor?"

"You still work in the reference department at the college library, don't you?"

"Sure."

He finished the milk and set the glass on the coffee table next to a stack of nineteenth century fiction journals. "To put it bluntly, I want you to help me steal a book from Special Collections."

She gaped at him. "I always thought you were a little strange. Now I know you're crazy. Nigel, that's in a different category from lending you my English notes when you fell asleep in class."

"This isn't how I'd have chosen to spend the weekend, either." He chuckled. "My guardian wants me to get possession of the book."

Nigel had no close family, as far as Denise knew, and she'd never met this shadowy guardian--whether uncle, great-uncle, or distant cousin--who was so lavish with material wealth and eccentric commands. "Then he's nuts, too," she said. But curiosity wouldn't let her drop the subject. "What book are you supposed to steal and why?"

"You know about the Ashleigh collection?"

"Of course." The college's acquisition of Winston Ashleigh's British incunabula and Colonial American publications, worth unspecified thousands of dollars, was a major triumph for William and Mary's library. Several university presses vied for the privilege of publishing a limited facsimile edition of selected books in the collection.

Nigel said, "The book my guardian's interested in happens to be one of those scheduled for the facsimile reprint series. My family has a reason for not wanting that particular book made public. Three other copies of the work are known to exist, and we have them all. The copy owned by the Ashleigh clan was no problem as long as it stayed locked in their private library. Now it's a different matter."

Nigel delivered this speech in such a serious tone that Denise really did wonder if he'd run off the rails. "Wonderful. You not only want me to help steal an old book, you want me to steal a rare and valuable old book."

"Come on, think of it as a harmless student prank."

"You preppies may call it a prank," she said. "We members of the bourgeoisie adhere to higher standards." Denise's private moral code counted violating the sanctity of a library as a sin slightly less heinous than murder.

What has the man done to me? I'm actually arguing this lame-brained notion as if there's some chance I'll cooperate.

He leaned forward, elbows resting on his knees, capturing her eyes with his own. Those incredible gray eyes-- "Won't you trust me on the importance of this, Denise?"

She felt dizzy for a second. She must not be completely awake yet. "Good grief, you're serious. I don't see you trusting me very far. You haven't told me what's so vital about this book."

"Fair point," he conceded. "After--if--we manage to get hold of it, I'll show you what's in it. If not, the whole question will be moot."

"What do you need me for, anyway? Do your own criminal work."

"You know the layout of the library. You can save me time and confusion. Also, you possess a car that's a lot less conspicuous than mine and has a William and Mary parking sticker."

"You're crazy," she persisted, though somehow her heart wasn't in the argument anymore. "There's not a snowball's chance of getting anything out of the Rare Books Room, much less out of the building."

"We can but try."

"And if we--you--don't succeed, I'm the one who gets thrown out of school and into jail."

"Oh, you won't get into trouble. I guarantee that."

That ridiculously casual assurance topped everything he'd said so far. *Why not humor him?* Denise thought. As soon as the attempt proved how hopeless his scheme was, he'd give up and leave.

"All right, anything to shut you up. We'd better hurry. The library closes at twelve on Fridays this time of year." She ducked into the bedroom for her purse and keys.

Nigel's smile hinted that he suspected the motive behind her sudden capitulation, but he held the door for her without a word. Outside, a cluster of mosquitoes orbited the porch light. The fragrance of honeysuckle hung thick in the air. A rabbit erupted from a forsythia bush and bolted for the woods.

"I like your location," said Nigel. "You have much wildlife this close to town?"

Denise shrugged. "Possums and raccoons. Sometimes a deer."

Both rabbits and felonies vanished from her thoughts at the sight of Nigel's car. A silver Corvette was parked behind her gas-hoarding, Junebug-green compact.

"Good Lord. I see what you mean by 'conspicuous'." Last time she'd seen Nigel, he'd been driving a Porsche. Who was that guardian of his, the Godfather?

"I'll take you for a ride later if there's time," he said complacently, opening the driver's door of her car for her.

"No, thanks. I remember how you drive!"

Once they were both belted in, she eased the car from the gravel-surfaced lane onto the main road and headed for the historic district. After turning the corner at a field bounded by a split-rail fence, she drove past a row of restored Georgian houses, the eighteenth-century powder magazine, and the back lot of the King's Arms.

"Speaking of trust," said Nigel, "the details of what I'm after aren't my secret to tell. Not without firmer justification."

"Like having a felony to hold over my head?"

"If you care to put it that way." He grinned.

Shortly they reached the triangle where the Jamestown and Yorktown highways made a V with Duke of Gloucester Street. The campus fanned back from the Christopher Wren building, focus of several brick-paved paths. Denise turned up the left arm of the V toward the newer buildings.

Pulling into the nearly deserted library parking lot, she said, "If you're not going to succumb to a sudden attack of sanity, you could at least tell me what we're looking for."

"Yes, of course. It's a book printed in 1497, written by an obscure English priest named Geoffrey Hillyard. The title translates from Latin as *A True Relation of the Portent Known as the Demon of Corville.*"

"This is so vital you have to steal it?" She twisted the ignition key with unnecessary force. "Never mind. Let's get this over with."

They entered through the turnstile at the circulation desk. Denise waved a greeting to her friend Joan at the check-out station, glad Joan was too busy with a patron to show curiosity about Nigel. Denise and Nigel crossed to the elevator, which was otherwise empty as they rode it down to the ground floor. Crossing the dimly lit circular lobby to the Rare Books Room, she found herself groping for his hand. His grip was firm and cool. Feeling her heartbeat accelerate, she knew her own palm must be damp. The larger-than-life statue of a Colonial Virginia governor that dominated the lobby seemed like an embodiment of her conscience.

"Don't be so nervous," Nigel said. "Your face fairly screams guilt."

She jumped. In the carpeted chamber, his low voice seemed to echo through the silence. "It's him." She nodded at the statue, trying to speak lightly. "A hostile *genius loci.*"

Nigel's gray eyes mocked her qualms.

"I just remembered, the Rare Books Room is closed by now," she whispered.

"Exactly why I brought you along. There's still a staff member on duty, isn't there?"

Denise nodded.

"Excellent. The doors won't be locked. We're using the back entrance, which you are going to show me."

"Nigel, where is your grip on reality tonight? Whoever's at the desk would hear us banging around in the back room for sure!" She had to fight to hold her voice to a furious whisper.

"I'll take care of that. Wait here."

He strode to the door and entered, leaving it ajar. Denise, lurking in the shadows and hoping the librarian--a middle-aged blonde woman she slightly knew--wouldn't notice her in the dim light of the lobby, watched Nigel walk up to the desk.

"Sir, we're closed until--"

"Terribly sorry to bother you, but I've driven all the way from Charlottesville. It's rather urgent."

Before Denise quite grasped how he'd gotten that far, he was sitting on the edge of the desk, turning the full candlepower of his smile on the bewildered librarian. Did he think masculine charm could bend the rules?

Yet, to Denise's surprise, the woman gazed at Nigel as if a strange man practically nesting in her Out Box were an everyday occurrence.

He lightly fingered a wisp of blonde hair snagged on the earpiece of her wire-rimmed glasses. "You'll make an exception this time, won't you?" he murmured.

The librarian blinked as if trying to break a trance and shook her head. Instead of giving up, Nigel lowered his voice to a croon whose words Denise couldn't distinguish. The woman gazed wide-eyed at him as he stroked her hair, the light touch becoming more blatantly a caress every minute. Gradually her lids drooped shut.

Though inwardly sizzling with irrational jealousy, Denise was too puzzled to interfere. She hadn't suspected Nigel of such refined skill in hypnosis.

He eased the woman's head onto the padded back of the swivel chair. "You will sleep for the next hour unless someone disturbs you earlier. Then you will wake naturally and lock up according to your usual routine. You won't remember meeting me. I was never here. Nobody was here."

Stepping back from the desk, he surveyed his work with evident satisfaction. He rejoined Denise and shut the door. "That should hold. Come on. We've no time to waste."

Automatically responding to his brisk tone, Denise led the way down the hall to the staff entrance. "Nigel, how did you hypnotize her so fast?"

He shrugged. "I'm a psych major."

Yes, but his specialty was theoretical, not clinical. And she'd never heard of a subject falling into a deep trance so promptly.

They tiptoed to the door of the work area behind the Rare Books Room. When Denise hesitated, Nigel said, "Relax, it's deserted--I don't hear anybody."

They stepped into the windowless room, hardly bigger than a walk-in closet. Nigel shut the door before turning on the overhead light. Denise inhaled the comfortable smell of dust, aged leather, and musty paper. Books were piled on the shelves lining each wall, along with a few electric typewriters and microfilm-reading machines. Five wooden crates sat in the middle of the floor.

"That would be the Ashleigh collection," said Denise. "You're really going through with this."

"Well, I didn't mesmerize the lady out there for the sheer pleasure of it."

She took a deep breath and glared at him. "This has gone far enough. A joke is a joke, but I'm ready to leave now."

He cupped her chin and stared into her eyes. Suddenly the foot of difference between their heights seemed to stretch until he loomed over her. "Denise, dear girl, you don't want to fight me on this, do you?"

She felt lightheaded. Of course she didn't want to resist him. She only wanted to drift in the misty gray of his eyes. *No! He's doing it to me now!* She jerked out of his grasp, and he didn't try to hold her.

"Forget it! You can't overpower me that easily."

"Worth a try," he said with a wry smile. "But you know that if you insist on leaving, I'll continue alone. And suppose I get caught and connected with you?"

"All right, you've got me there." Her curiosity about the books fought with her indignation and won. She knelt beside the nearest box.

"Damn, there's a lot here," Nigel said. "This could take a while." She expected him to pry off the lid with a knife. Instead, he simply gripped the edge with both hands and tugged. The top peeled off like cardboard. Nigel winced at the rending sound. "Noisy, too. Let's hope there's nobody prowling the halls."

Denise goggled at him.

With a frown of impatience, he scooped out the first layer of Styrofoam popcorn. "Let's get to it. We don't have all night. You're looking for a small volume, quite old, in Latin. Show me any possibilities you come across."

Wrenching herself out of her momentary paralysis, she sat on the floor beside him and began pawing through the box. In spite of the dust tickling her nose, she succumbed to the lure of mildewed bindings and faded ink. She wished they did have all night to pore over this trove.

Nigel echoed her sentiments. "I do lust after that book, but I won't be allowed to use it in my research."

"Demons? What could that possibly have to do with your field?"

"I'm working on psychohistory, remember? This illustrates a turning point in cultural attitudes toward the supernatural. Tell you about it later."

After delving to the bottom of the first crate, he opened a second, and later a third. Denise's back ached by now, but she'd pushed guilt to the bottom of her mind and surrendered to the pleasure of the quest.

Finally Nigel emitted a suppressed cry of triumph. "Here it is! And none too soon." As she started to rise from the floor, he grabbed her arm. "Quiet. Oh, hell, someone's coming."

A few seconds later, she, too, heard footsteps in the hall.

Nigel leaped up to extinguish the light, then crouched beside her. "Stay down, out of sight, and out of my way. I won't be any rougher than minimally necessary."

In the unrelieved darkness she heard Nigel creeping toward the door. How did he keep from stumbling over boxes?

From the hall a man's voice said, "Who's in there? Is everything okay?"

He shoved open the door. In the light from the corridor Denise caught a glimpse of a security guard's uniform. She absorbed no other details about the man, except that, although shorter than Nigel, he was twice as broad.

The guard stepped inside, raising a flashlight. "I know somebody's in here--might as well show yourself."

Just as he flicked on his light, Nigel loomed up behind him. The flash dropped from the guard's hand as Nigel's fist descended on the back of his neck. The man hit the floor with a muted groan and a thud.

Nigel wasn't even breathing hard. "He didn't get a look at us. Your reputation is safe."

She tiptoed to his side. Unlike Nigel, she felt herself on the verge of hyperventilating. She gulped. "He isn't dead?"

"I told you I wouldn't seriously hurt him. For heaven's sake, calm down. We still have to get out of here with our prize."

He clasped her hand to lead her into the hall.

Squinting in the light, she checked her watch. "Guess what, the library's closed."

"I wasn't planning to walk out the front door, anyway. Where are the nearest stairs?"

She guided him around several corners to a glowing Exit sign. Climbing to the first floor, they emerged in the reference section. She glanced around this familiar territory, relieved to find no one in sight.

But Nigel lifted his head like a startled deer. "Stay in contact with me and freeze," he whispered.

Startled by his urgent tone, she obeyed. Then she heard wheels on the carpet. A book cart, pushed by a young black man, appeared between the stacks. He was headed straight for their corner.

Denise held her breath while Nigel squeezed her hand. Watching his face, she saw his eyes unfocus as if he were falling into a trance. The cart rattled closer. The man--Bob, that was his name--couldn't fail to see them. Denise's mind scrambled for excuses why she'd be giving a friend a tour of the library after closing.

Bob strolled past, within arm's reach. His eyes slid right over them.

When he'd disappeared out of sight and earshot, Denise let out her breath. "He didn't see us. He looked right at us, but he didn't see us."

"Just preoccupied, no doubt."

Denise snorted at this feeble rationalization.

"Nobody else in the area," said Nigel. "Our luck's holding. Are the windows alarmed?"

"Not yet. They don't set the alarms until they lock up and leave."

Nigel strode to the nearest window, unlatched it, and pushed it up. "Too easy. The security system could use overhauling."

He moved a chair for Denise to stand on. When she mounted it and stood irresolute, her hands on the sill, he gave her a light slap on the rear.

"Don't lose your nerve now."

In that position, the window was at her waist level, so it was easy, albeit awkward, for her to drag herself through the opening. She scraped her forearm on the latch.

Nigel followed, closing the window behind them. "Clumsy," he said amiably. "You've hurt yourself." He took her hand and examined the laceration, which was beading blood. "Get that cleaned up as soon as you can. Don't want infection."

"I'm perfectly capable of taking care of myself," she said, "when not being dragged around on illegal expeditions by nutty friends."

She found they were standing on the roof of a jutting portion of the ground level set into a hillside. Kneeling next to the low concrete wall, she saw that the drop to the pavement was at least twice her height. She turned to face Nigel. In the dark his eyes glowed crimson at the centers.

Hallucination, she insisted to herself. Or a trick of the light. *No. Flash bulbs can make human eyes shine red; ordinary light can't. So it's hallucination.*

Abruptly Nigel pulled her close, nuzzled her scratched arm, and kissed her hard on the lips. After a second of shock, she melted in response. In contrast to his cool hands, his lips burned.

He released her just as suddenly. "Sorry. Couldn't resist. It won't happen again."

Why not? she inwardly raged.

Before she could gather her wits, he wrapped his arms around her. Her head spun as he lifted her and leaped off the roof as casually as if jumping into a swimming pool. She closed her eyes. Instead of a jarring drop, she felt as if they were floating through the air. *Maybe I'm catching some kind of virus. Or he did hypnotize me after all.* She ventured a peek.

Nigel landed, catlike, without a jolt. They were standing in the parking lot. When he set her down, she again noticed the red gleam in his eyes. *No, I don't,* she insisted.

He looked around and cocked his head as if listening. "The coast is clear, Watson."

"I don't see you as Holmes," she sniffed. "I think you're actually having fun."

"Most I've had all year." He took her arm and walked her to the car. "How's your Latin?"

"Rusty. I don't have much call to use it in real life."

"What's the world coming to?" he sighed with a head-shake of mock despair. "All right. You drive, and I'll read to you." He held up the book. In the parking lot floodlight she noticed it was a leather-bound octavo volume with brass guards at each corner of the cover.

Denise didn't breathe deeply until they were well away from the library, safely moving in the direction of home.

Nigel gave her a sly smile. "Glad it's over? According to the Marquis de Sade, it's only the first crime that's difficult. Before you know it, you'll be a hardened malefactor."

"Oh, shut up, Nigel. Unless you're going to tell me about the book, the way you promised."

"Right." He opened it, turning pages one by one with a scholar's care. "This Father Hillyard was the village priest in a little place called Corville, north of London. There was an outbreak of assaults in the area, attributed to some sort of demonic creature. Hillyard investigated, and interviewed some of the victims. Unfortunately, the situation was never resolved. The locals marched on the castle where the 'demon' supposedly laired, but there was no flaming Hollywood climax. The creature had disappeared. Hillyard linked this episode with a local legend, similar attacks on young women that had taken place around the year 1100. But the bishop censured him because of the unorthodox conclusions he reached. That's why there are so few copies left. Listen to this."

He read slowly, translating. "I believe that the 'monstrum'--either 'portent' or 'monster' in the modern sense--said to have inhabited the abandoned castle of the Corvilles is the same being that dwelt there four centuries ago. If so, this long life argues that he is indeed a fiend from the Abyss. Yet I believe otherwise. I conversed at length with the only maiden to be taken to the castle and imprisoned there for a long period, and then to escape. Having passed some seven weeks in his company, she holds that the Demon is no hellish spirit, but a creature of flesh, bound by the laws of his nature, though it be different from ours."

"Sounds more like science fiction than demonology," said Denise.

"Father Hillyard, poor fellow, had a surprisingly modern outlook." Nigel read on, "In the ensuing pages I shall demonstrate by many and weighty proofs my reasons for upholding this belief. To wit: Though the Demon did indeed, by the maiden's testimony, drink her blood from minute cuts on her neck or arm, he also fed upon the blood of deer and other game, and also upon milk brought to him by his agents, certain lawless men in his hire. She never observed him to change shape as devilish spirits are said to do, save that for the purpose of flight, he was wont to sprout a pair of great wings. He passed through doors by opening them, in the manner of a mortal. Though his strength was prodigious, it was no greater than that of wild creatures such as wolves and bears. He hungered, grew weary, and could be hurt, like a mortal. Nor did the Demon catch fire and crumble to ash in the rays of the sun, as has been idly rumored. She saw him abroad by daylight more than once, though he confessed that he avoided the sun because it distressed him."

Denise pulled the car behind the Corvette in front of her house and stared at Nigel. The look he gave her before continuing showed that he realized the wild notion burgeoning in her brain.

"For these and many other reasons, I hold that the so-called Demon who scourged this region both four centuries ago and these past few years was no fiend, but a creature of another race, with the outward form of man, yet with certain differences from human nature. I believe that he ought to be classed with the longaevi--" He broke off and said to Denise, "You know that word, of course? the 'long-lived ones'." He read on, "--like the fauns, nymphs, and satyrs of the ancient world, or with the folk of the Antipodes told of in travelers' tales, neither human nor beast, yet creatures of this earth, spawned in neither Heaven nor Hell. Moreover, if this one exists, surely others of his kind must dwell somewhere, for they must breed, however infrequently." He closed the book and laid it between their seats.

"Your family wants this suppressed?" said Denise. "What's the point? Nobody would believe it except the lunatic fringe."

Nigel nodded. "Some of those would, certainly--the type of people who read Fort and Von Daniken with relish, the type who hanker to believe in gods from outer space, strange creatures living secretly among humankind, and all sorts of monstrous conspiracies. But there's another category that would accept Father Hillyard's theory as fact. The few people who've met such creatures and suffered at their hands--or think they have. These people are isolated now." He smiled wryly at the way Denise half-consciously drew back against the driver's door. "Those who believe in these creatures and want revenge for real or imagined injuries would jump at any scrap of published proof, however farfetched. They'd welcome the chance to get together with others who share their obsession. They might even manage to convince a measurable percentage of the public that they aren't so nutty after all."

For a minute they silently stared at each other in the moonlight. Nigel remained motionless, a faint smile on his lips, like a man trying to tame a wary animal. His breathing was labored, from excitement, Denise sensed, not exertion. Again she glimpsed a red gleam in his eyes. This time she didn't try to fool herself that she imagined it. She recalled how he'd hypnotized the librarian, made the two of them virtually invisible, and made that incredible leap from the roof with her in his arms.

Finally she burst out, "Nigel--what are you?"

He took a deep breath before speaking. "What would you call a creature that lives for thousands of years, avoids sunlight, sometimes lapses into suspended animation during the day, can be killed only with great difficulty, has superhuman strength, speed, and endurance, as well as certain powers ordinarily called 'psychic', and subsists mainly on blood?"

"If this is a riddle, what's the punch line?"

"There's an easy one-word answer. But it's misleading."

"Vampire, I suppose."

"Close enough," he said. "But not a walking corpse or spawn of the Devil. Just another species, a minority passing for human, not daring to let their true nature be known."

Her fear was swamped by the indignation she still hadn't worked through. "Damn you. Why did you have to make me your accomplice? You could have handled this whole thing just fine by yourself. You and your superhuman powers!"

"But having you along made it so much easier. Believe it or not, I really wanted to avoid violence." He rubbed his eyes. "Look, could we fight in the house? This is a damned uncomfortable car you've got."

He stepped out of the car. The moment he shut the passenger door, Denise pushed the automatic lock button, revved the engine, and backed up in a shower of gravel. She spun around and roared up to the main road. She fleetingly wondered what she would do if Nigel grabbed her door handle or jumped in front of the car. He made no move to stop her, though. Luckily, no traffic was nearby when she reached the corner; she could make a right turn without pausing.

She'd driven almost fifteen minutes, with no sign of Nigel's Corvette pursuing, when she started to calm down. Easing back on the accelerator, she scanned the roadside until she noticed a picnic area. She pulled into the turn-off and sat there, trembling, for another five minutes.

How she wished she could think Nigel was out of his mind. But that would make her crazy, too, because she'd seen him do those peculiar things. And the revelation fit so well with the oddities she'd observed in him through the years. His mainly nocturnal schedule, his avoidance of the sun, the way she'd never seen him eat solid food--he gave allergies and poor health as excuses, yet he was the most vibrant, energetic person she'd ever met. After dark he was, anyway.

Why did he let me notice tonight? He could have made sure I didn't.

She switched on the interior dome light and picked up the leather-bound book. Her Latin was as rusty as she'd told Nigel. Skimming the first few pages, she distinguished enough words to confirm that he'd translated accurately. She leafed through the rest of the volume.

The word "incensa"--burned--caught her eye. Frowning at the faded print, she read from the top of the page. The passage seemed to tell the "local legend" of a woman who'd spent months as the Demon's captive around the year 1100. This girl, Isobel, had somehow escaped and returned home. Instead of staying with her family, though, she had rejoined the Demon of her own free will. This choice brought her the reputation of heresy, Satan-worship, and witchcraft. When a plague of some kind struck the town, she and her "Demon Lord" were blamed. Villagers, led by the priest, had invaded the castle by day and captured Isobel. They burned her to death. The Demon had wreaked a bloody vengeance on the murderers, then vanished until four centuries later.

Denise realized her hands were shaking again as she put the book aside. *Am I supposed to believe this fairy tale? No, more like a horror story.*

Nigel seemed to believe that the tale held some truth. He apparently trusted her to understand, or at least suspend judgment.

He's never hurt me. He could have forced me to help him, but he left me a choice.

And he hadn't chased her down, as he easily could have. Her compact would've been no match for his Corvette. She decided she owed him a hearing, if nothing else. She pulled onto the highway and headed for home.

Nigel waited on her porch, leaning on the rail with his arms folded. He watched while she walked to the front door and made awkward stabs at the lock with her key. The cloud of mosquitoes around the bare light bulb had thickened. Denise noticed how none of them paid any attention to Nigel. He kept silent until she got the door open.

As they entered the living room, he said, "Decided I'm not going to eat you alive?"

She slammed and bolted the door. "You could've hypnotized me into forgetting the whole thing. Why didn't you? It would have been so much easier!"

"I considered it." He stood in the middle of the rug, watching her.

She spun around to face him. "You did hypnotize me, didn't you? At the beginning, to make me go along with your scheme!"

"I gave you a slight nudge, that's all. I couldn't bring myself to do anything more drastic. I've never liked deceiving you. Maybe I half-consciously wanted you to notice my--differences--wanted you to discover the truth."

"Spoken like a true psychologist," she sniffed.

"Confound it, I do care about you! I've always thought of you as a friend, and I don't want that to change."

She flung her purse and keys on the couch. "And how do you think of the rest of the human race? Domestic animals?"

"For the most part," he said. "Should I lie? If I'm going to start telling you the truth, I don't want to settle for half measures." He perched on one arm of the couch.

She took a seat at the other end. Her anger yielded to curiosity. "Nigel, how old are you?"

He laughed. "Don't jump to any grandiose conclusions. I'm in my early thirties, not much older than I look." He scanned her disheveled form. "You're still upset about being pressured into violating your conscience."

"What did you think, I'd get over it? But I guess human standards don't mean anything to you."

"Of course they do," he said patiently. "I've been exposed to them most of my life. And I do have my own ethics, though they might strike you as a bit skewed."

"Like how to treat friends?"

"Among other things. You see, we know only one way to express affection. I couldn't be intimate with you without--tasting you--and I couldn't tell you about myself without some compelling reason. So to avoid a situation where I'd have to deceive you, I kept you at a distance."

"I think I see." Her head buzzed with confusion. *He left me alone because he cared about me. Isn't that one of the Ten Standard Lines?*

"Look, would it make you feel better if I sent an anonymous donation to the college, enough to cover the artifact's value?"

"Maybe. I don't know."

"It's the principle, isn't it? Very well. If you're positive you want the book returned, I'll do it tomorrow night, at whatever risk."

Was he making a sincere offer or manipulating her again? "What would your guardian think about that?"

"He wouldn't quite flay me alive," said Nigel with a sardonic smile. "It would just feel as if he had. But consider carefully--Do you really want this material published? Do you want the world to know about us? I'm not saying that outcome is certain, but it's more than possible. Back in 1100, there was a girl. Isobel--"

"I read that part. It's true?"

"Yes. She wasn't even one of us, just condemned by association. And we can be killed. Decapitation--dismemberment--cremation--total destruction of the brain--it's difficult, but not impossible." Sensing her revulsion, apparently, he continued more gently, "I'm not trying to terrify you. Not much, anyhow. But don't fool yourself that it couldn't happen today. The only difference would be in greater efficiency. Vampires have been killed as such in twentieth-century America. I am not overdramatizing."

Denise suppressed a shiver. "All right. Do what you have to." She felt as if the words were choking her.

He squeezed her hand. "I knew I could trust you."

Had she decided correctly? She was still an accessory to theft. On the other hand, Nigel had taken a serious risk in telling her the truth. How could she betray him? The act was done, and she resolved to stop agonizing over it. "Just don't forget that anonymous donation."

Nigel leaned back wearily on the couch. "It's getting late. Much as I dislike the idea, I've got to leave."

"You aren't going to drive back to Charlottesville tonight, are you?"

"Hardly. I'll get a motel room for the day."

She felt her heart racing and had to force the next sentence past her constricted throat. "You could stay here. This couch is a hide-a-bed."

His eyes widened in surprise. "You're still a little afraid of me. I feel it."

She swallowed a momentary queasiness. "I'd be an idiot not to have some fear of the unknown. But I trust you."

"You shouldn't," said Nigel crisply. "That comes from ignorance. In my present condition I don't dare stay near you."

"You mean--?"

"I'm hungry," he said with a quiet emphasis more convincing than histrionics. "I have to feed before daybreak. Earlier in the evening I didn't manage to score--as my cruder contemporaries would say--and I had to give up in order to leave myself enough time to drive here. The stress I've been under since then has put an edge on my appetite." He forced a smile. "You can't imagine how close you came to getting ravished on the library roof."

She sensed that his deliberate bluntness was meant to put her off. Yet with each passing second her qualms diminished. This was just Nigel, after all, whatever his peculiarities.

"How much do you take?"

"Difficult to estimate. Normally about four ounces."

"But that's nothing," she said, almost disappointed. *And here I was gearing up for some terrific sacrifice.*

"Our basic nutritional needs are supplied by animal blood and milk," he explained. "Think of human blood for us like trace elements in your own diet. Small in quantity but essential to life. That's misleading, too, though, because the need is more psychic than physical. Human blood is more than food and drink. It's a substitute for sex, and something very much like a drug. An addictive craving that strikes with the onset of puberty and recurs every few days for the rest of our lives."

She edged closer to him. "Does it hurt? The victim, I mean."

"Please--donor. It isn't supposed to."

"That's not a very responsive answer."

He smiled at her persistence. "It hurts only if the vampire is a sadist or an insensitive clod."

"I know that doesn't describe you." She reached up to smooth the hair curling over his forehead. "I'm healthy--want to see my Red Cross blood bank card? And I haven't been eating pizza. Or is the garlic business a myth?"

"Oh, that part is true enough. But it's not a screaming terror, just a very severe allergy. And I don't need proof of your health. It's obvious."

"What about it, then? You don't need to suffer when I'm right here."

He sat rigid as if fighting not to touch her. "Denise, what you're offering would not be wise."

She pulled back. If he expected her to do all the seducing, he could forget it. "All right, if you don't want--"

He grabbed her wrists painfully hard. "For God's sake, don't tease! I can't handle it."

"I'm not!" she gasped.

He stood up and jerked her to her feet. "You really mean it, don't you? What the hell. I may be out of my mind, but I accept."

His arms encircled her, and his mouth descended upon hers. After the first few seconds, the harshness of the kiss faded into lingering sensuality. Again she felt the searing heat of his lips. The room blurred to silken darkness around her. He released her only on the verge of fainting.

He let go and stepped back so abruptly that she almost fell. "Tone that down a bit, will you," he said huskily. "Take a couple of slow, deep breaths. That's right--that way you automatically decelerate your heartbeat, too. Better."

He lightly clasped her upper arms. Shivering despite the muggy air, she noticed for the first time that the palms of his hands bristled against her skin.

"You do have hairs in the centers of your palms," she said.

"Cilia, technically," Nigel said. "Something like a cat's whiskers." He gently hugged her to his chest. "I've fantasized about this for years. Damned if I'll be provoked into wasting it on three minutes in the middle of your living room."

"Then you do want to take me to bed?" she said in delighted wonder.

"The bed is optional. Saves me the bother of picking you up when you collapse."

Glimpsing the amused quirk of his lips, in retaliation she slipped her fingers inside his collar and dug in her nails. His arms tightened again, and his breathing roughened.

"Stop that! I will not be rushed. It would be like going to the King's Arms and ordering the diet plate."

Denise laughed at the image of a velvet-coated servitor at the restored Colonial tavern ceremoniously presenting a dollop of cottage cheese on a lettuce leaf. But then Nigel kissed her again, setting her head awhirl.

He gazed down into her eyes. "My dear girl, one reason I hesitated was because I can't offer you the exclusive commitment we'll both want."

She stiffened. "Did I ask for one?"

He kissed her forehead. "Sorry. I put that badly. Not a social commitment, an involuntary one. If I drink from you often enough--and it doesn't take much--I'll be fixated on you. It's a trap perilously easy to fall into, as if nature intended us for an exclusive bond with one donor. And you'll be addicted, too. It works both ways. The catch is, it couldn't be exclusive, because our academic obligations will keep us apart. A double bind I could do without. I can't stay away from you, though." The sigh that ruffled her hair seemed to convey more pleasure than frustration over being caught in that "bind".

"Then you're not talking one-night stand? You will visit me again?"

"Regularly. As often as I can."

She snuggled to his chest. "Then that's what I want. Even if I do have to deal with this 'addiction'. We'll work it out."

"Then that's enough. It's a beginning."

He picked her up and carried her to the bedroom.

(Story originally published in *Good Guys Wear Fangs 1*, 1992)

PART II
ELVES AND OTHER
HEART'S DESIRES

Heart's Desire

The night her husband Tom spoke of dying, Rachel decided to visit the witch.

As usual, he limped into the cottage at evening, greeted Rachel and the children with an unsmiling monosyllable, and ate a bowl of stew in silence. When little Tommy edged up to him and said, "Da, can you make me a boat to sail in the pond?" he gave the expected answer.

"Not tonight, lad. Maybe some other day." Though never rough with the children, he always spoke in that distant manner, as if he hardly saw them.

Poor Will, at only four years old, didn't know his father had ever been different, had no memory of the old Tom. Before the accident three years past, Tom had laughed and tumbled with the children and often whittled toys for them out of scraps from the woodshed.

Rachel blinked back tears as she sent the little ones up to the loft to prepare for bed under the care of Kate, the oldest. Tom drank his usual three tall mugs of ale, while Rachel watched him from the corner of her eye as she cleared the dishes and scoured the pot. After she climbed the ladder to say goodnight to the children, she returned to the common room to find Tom already stripped and stretched on the bed in the corner.

The light from the one candle she'd left burning showed that at least he was still awake. Thankfully she peeled off her clothes, quickly washed her face and arms in the water basin, and lay down beside him. *I must keep trying, or he'll lose all faith in his manhood.*

With a long, ragged sigh, he threw one arm over his eyes, hiding from her.

"Tom--sweet--" She ran her fingers over his chest, still as hard and smooth as ever, except for a ridged scar under one rib. A tingle ran up her arm. Even after three years of disappointment, she couldn't help hungering for him. She pressed against him, touching her lips to his bare shoulder. He shivered. Her nipples tightened at contact with his warm flesh.

"It's no use--" he murmured.

"Hush, love." Her fingertips skimmed over his belly; she felt the muscles grow taut. Gently she savored the heat of his loins, cupping the heaviness of his testicles. Her flesh heated in response to his stifled moan. She ventured up to grasp his cock. Maybe this time--

But all her caresses brought forth no more than a faint stir. It lay asleep in her hand.

She kneaded his thighs, avoiding the scars that marked the injured leg. He shifted restlessly, as if impatient with her exertions. She curled around him to plant kisses on his cheek, shoulders, and chest, tasting the salt of his sweat. Drawing her leg across his, she reveled in the friction of the coarse hair on her tender skin. *Why doesn't he try harder? Doesn't he even want to make love anymore?* Again she fingered his limp penis.

With a groan, he rolled on top and fastened his mouth to hers. His tongue probed her lips. Wrapping her arms around him, she kneaded the firm muscles of his shoulders. His organ felt like a hot coal pressed against her groin. But it remained soft. Rocking her hips, Rachel struggled to force the tip of his cock to press against the maddeningly tickle between her legs.

Tom withdrew and turned on his stomach. Massaging his back, she felt him shaking. He shrugged her off with as much animation as a puppet.

"Tom, don't--"

"I should have died that day." His voice sounded thick with tears. "I'm good for nothing. Should've died."

Seconds later, he fell asleep--or passed out, from the quantity of ale he'd drunk.

A flood of moisture suffused Rachel's quim. Tears leaked from her closed eyes as she stroked the damp curls between her legs. Her fingers stole to the swollen nub of flesh that quivered with eagerness at her own touch. It throbbed, starved for attention. She stroked from top to bottom of her slit, lingering each time on the aching spot at the peak. Faster and faster she rubbed, until her body convulsed in release.

She bit down on a sob, for fear of waking the children. She hadn't gotten married just to twiddle her own privates like a lovesick girl, while her husband snored beside her. *Why don't I stop trying to beguile him? Then I wouldn't have to feel this pain.*

A new, frightening idea came to her: *Why should I not take a lover, as any man would?* But that was out of the question, in their small community. *Everyone would know, and I would lose my children, my freedom, perhaps my life. I could never do it, even if there were any man hereabouts who roused my lust. Even if I could bear to hurt Tom.*

Before the accident, he'd been a vigorous lover, and she'd delighted in their coupling, even though the delights he enjoyed always eluded her unless she'd supplemented his thrusting with her own fingers. Still, he had at least tried to please her with his mouth and hands, although with an enthusiasm more clumsy than skillful.

Since the fall three years ago, he hadn't even tried. He behaved as if he felt afraid or ashamed of any loving contact, as if any embrace or caress would make his failure all the more obvious.

And now this talk of dying. Fear grew on top of Rachel's habitual sorrow and bitterness. Before, she'd persuaded herself that Tom would get better. Now she had to face the hollowness of that hope.

When he'd fallen while mending a high roof, cracking his skull and breaking a leg, she'd thought his very survival a miracle. The Baron had sent his own physician, who had informed them nothing could be done but keep the injured man quiet and pray for God's grace. The priest, Father Joseph, had even administered the last rites. Yet Tom had lived.

Over the following months, eggs from the henhouse, the profits of Rachel's weaving, and aid from her widowed Aunt Judith had kept the family from ruin. Against all probability, Tom's slurred speech had returned to normal, the palsy in his right side had disappeared, and the fractured leg had healed with only a slight limp. True, he could no longer manage delicate work, but otherwise he returned to his carpentry and provided for his wife and children as always.

The months of helplessness, though, had destroyed his spirit. He moved and spoke like a wooden effigy of a man. And since the injury he'd never once achieved a cockstand. Perhaps he saw Rachel's attempts at lovemaking as further humiliation.

I can't let him--or myself--go on this way any longer. I've no choice; I must appeal to Mistress Susanna.

While Susanna plied a legitimate trade in herbal remedies and healing salves, the whole village knew of her more dubious skills. As long as no one spoke that knowledge aloud, the priest didn't have to take official notice.

Rachel had gone to her once, ten months after little Will's birth, when she'd found herself pregnant too soon. She knew that if the new pregnancy dried up her milk, Will would have small chance of survival. Babes deprived of mother's milk too early tended to succumb to fevers or simply waste away. So Rachel had purchased a dose to empty her womb, letting Tom believe the loss was a natural miscarriage. Had he known the truth, he might have felt hurt, thinking his manhood slighted.

Since the accident, Rachel sometimes wondered whether the injury might be God's punishment for her lack of faith shown by killing her unborn child. *No, He couldn't be so cruel. Where would be the sense in punishing Tom and all our children for a small sin of mine?* Many women ended their pregnancies for one reason or another, and the Church turned a blind eye as long as quickening hadn't yet begun.

Having talked herself into visiting the witch the very next day, Rachel relaxed into sleep.

Tom left home early the next morning, for an all-day job rebuilding a fence for the butcher. His absence gave Rachel the perfect opportunity to carry out her plan. Leaving Kate in charge of the other children, she set out for Mistress Susanna's cottage with a market basket over her arm. She stopped to make purchases at the fruit stall, to cover her true goal.

The witch's home lay at the end of a tree-shaded lane on the edge of the village. Despite the isolation, on a sultry summer day with sunlight dancing through the leaves it shouldn't have seemed frightening. Yet Rachel shivered as she stepped to the door, under an overhanging oak, and knocked. Everyone knew that magic, even white magic, held unpredictable dangers.

The half-forgotten scents of the cottage enveloped her the moment the door opened--a spicy, floral mixture like the fragrances from a noblewoman's kitchen or bower. A ginger cat stalked out of her path as Rachel tiptoed inside. She blinked for a minute, adjusting to the dimmer light in the room.

Susanna looked no different from their previous encounter. Although old enough to be Rachel's mother, she had a luxuriant bosom and glossy chestnut hair--and all her teeth, a sign of occult power in itself.

Rachel shivered again at the cool clasp of the witch's hand. "It's been a long time, child. Are you so afraid of me?"

Rachel blushed. To confess fear would be discourteous when she'd come to ask for help. "Please accept this small gift, Mistress Susanna." She placed three apples from her basket on the table.

Susanna inclined her head in thanks. "Come and sit down, my girl, and tell me what brings you here." She led the way to a pair of chairs by the open window. Her skirts rustled like leaves in a spring breeze.

A blackbird perched on a stand next to the window. Nervously glancing up at it, Rachel took the seat indicated. The smell of the cottage tickled her nose. She couldn't decide what it resembled--cinnamon? mint? roses? It differed completely from the comfortably musty odors of her own house, so familiar she hardly noticed them. This fragrance made her lightheaded, made her heart flutter with pleasurable excitement.

Susanna touched her hand again, making her heartbeat race still faster. "Tell me your troubles, while I fix you a cup of herb tea."

Rachel twisted her hands together in her lap. "You know about my husband Tom? How he had that fall three years ago and almost died?"

Lifting the simmering kettle from the hearth, Susanna nodded.

Rachel explained the aftereffects, stammering and casting down her eyes as she spoke of Tom's lost virility. "I tried to tell Aunt Judith about it once. She just told me to continue doing my wifely duty and be thankful my man was alive. She said what happened to him was God's will."

The witch sniffed. "Father Joseph and his devotees have a different idea about God's will from mine, that's clear. I hold that God has given us the wit to help ourselves." She handed Rachel a cup, delicately adorned with a pattern of ferns and violets. Sweet-scented steam arose from it.

Rachel sipped the hot drink, feeling its warmth spread through her body with the first taste. Her breasts and thighs tingled, as if invisible fingers had brushed them.

"Now, Rachel, what do you want from me? Is it only your husband's failure in bed that concerns you? You could find a lusty lad with a stiff prick to fill that need."

Rachel turned hot at the reminder of her own sinful speculations. "It's everything." Tears stung her eyes. "I can't stand to see Tom in such pain. He isn't himself anymore. The man I married has vanished. He's like a changeling. And now he says he wants to die--" With a trembling hand, she set aside the cup for fear of spilling it. She gave way to the sobs welling up in her throat.

Susanna's hand rested on her shoulder, then moved up to rub the back of her bowed neck. The strong, yet gentle touch sent shudders of pleasure through Rachel, in the midst of her sadness. She felt a strange confusion at this reaction to another woman.

"It's clear from what you've said, that your Tom is too far gone for any simple remedy. Yet there is something I might try, if you'll trust me. A potion I can brew, that may give you your heart's desire."

Rachel lifted her head and blinked through the shimmer of tears. *My heart's desire? That's too wild a promise to be true!* "The man I married?" she said. "Whole again, happy and loving the way I remember him?"

"And more," said the witch, "if you trust me."

"What else can I do? I have nowhere else to turn."

"Very well." Susanna crossed the room to a locked chest, which she opened to remove a number of vials and small boxes. "I shall brew the potion.

You must get Tom to drink it without telling him what you're doing. He would not accept any medicine if he knew it came from me. Men don't trust women's magic."

Rachel nodded eagerly. Her instincts had told her that truth when she'd bought the abortion dose.

Susanna closed the shutters and glided like a shadow in the undulant light from the hearth. After pouring a small portion of water into a clean pot, which she suspended over the fire, she cast in powders and liquids, so many different ingredients Rachel lost count. All the while, the witch hummed a tune like none Rachel had heard before.

Her eyes drooped. The cloud of steam that permeated the room imbued her with a dreamy, floating sensation. Inhaling the peculiar sweet-sour aroma of the brew, she felt a tingle beneath her skin like the scurrying feet of a thousand insects. She found herself stroking her thighs through the fabric of her skirt and apron.

Some time later, she opened her eyes with a start. Susanna had unfastened the shutters. Rachel watched her lift the pot, her hands wrapped in thick cloths, and pour the liquid into a vial.

"It will cool quickly," she murmured. "Think of your husband, my child. Imagine him as you want him to be, as he would be if you had your deepest desire."

Again closing her eyes, Rachel visualized Tom's straw-colored hair silken and sun-gold, as when he'd courted her. She saw his long, free stride and imagined the strong embrace of his arms. And his tongue on her nipples, his hands exploring her inner secrets, his erect organ--

She felt a hot blush on her face and bosom. Susanna's voice distracted her.

"There, it is done."

The witch picked up the vial. A blue glow flared around it. A heaviness filled the air, like an impending thunderstorm; Rachel thought she glimpsed miniature lightnings in the potion bottle. An answering thickness settled in her loins. She sighed aloud as Susanna pressed the vial into her hand. A ripple of sensation traveled from the witch's hand along Rachel's nerves.

When she looked closely at the vial, the blue glow and the sparks had vanished. It looked like water tinted lavender.

"If you mix this into his evening posset, he won't be able to taste it," Susanna said. "Whatever happens, don't be afraid. Have faith, and you will win your desire."

Rachel stood, tucking the vial in the bottom of her basket. She prayed her trembling legs would carry her home without advertising her excitement to all the neighbors. "I--I have nothing to pay you with today. Later, as soon as--"

The witch stopped her with a finger on her lips, a touch as soft as a mother's--or a lover's. "Nonsense. I ask no payment for this. It's but my duty to a woman in need."

A bit of luck came Rachel's way, a message from Aunt Judith that she'd fallen ill with a summer ague and wanted Kate's help for a night or two. Rachel gladly sent her daughter to tend the old woman. Now there'd be no fear of the girl's waking and asking questions when the magic worked. Rachel didn't know exactly what the potion would do and had no reason to think it would cause a disturbance. But she had no grounds for believing it wouldn't, either.

She tucked the younger children into their pallets in the loft as soon as they finished supper. She could trust them to sleep once they got settled. Tom came home from his chore at the butcher's, weary and taciturn as usual. She served him a heaping bowl of stew and the customary tankard of ale. She wanted him relaxed and muzzy before she tried to administer the potion, in case Mistress Susanna had been wrong about its tastelessness.

While he was hunched over the table, Rachel poured the contents of the vial into a mug, which she filled with cider. The tart flavor should disguise any taste the witch's medicine might have. Rachel's hand shook when she set the mug in front of Tom. Gnawing her lip, she prayed he wouldn't notice anything strange about her behavior and refuse the drink.

Of course he wouldn't. He had no reason to suspect her plan; only her own guilt made her nervous. *Can it be right to dose him with magic, even white magic, without his knowledge or will?* Too late now; the deed was done, and it was for his own good.

He muttered thanks for the cider and took a swig. Impulsively Rachel leaned over to kiss him on the lips. His felt like clay. He gave her a faintly puzzled look and turned his head to gulp the rest of the drink.

Rachel drew back, knotting her hands in the folds of her apron. He set down the mug and belched. For a moment he didn't move. His face turned stony, blank as the features of a marble saint in the parish church. Slowly he pulled himself to his feet. Opening his mouth, he took one step toward Rachel. He swayed, and a gurgle welled up from his throat. He crumpled to the floor.

She lurched forward and fell to her knees beside him. "No--Tom, wake up!" She forced herself to whisper; the children mustn't hear, mustn't see this. "Tom!" She kneaded his shoulders and groped for the pulse at his neck.

She felt a vibration under her hands. Blue fire sprang to life, a halo surrounding Tom's body. Rachel jumped back. The light licked over him, bathing every inch of his frame. Staring, she crammed her fist into her mouth to keep from screaming. The tongues of light coalesced into a glowing mist that grew denser until it hid his body altogether. Now she saw only a scintillating blue-violet cloud.

She backed against the wall, crossing herself over and over, too stunned to pray or cry out. Within a minute or two, the mist thinned, showing a ghostly outline of Tom's supine body. Then the blue flame gathered itself into a single shaft that speared toward the ceiling, like a lightning bolt crackling upward.

Rachel fought the paralysis of terror, inching toward the inert form. Again she pawed his chest and neck in search of a heartbeat. Nothing.

She choked down the cry that threatened to burst from her. *He can't be dead! What went wrong?* Had the witch played her false? Why? Or was this catastrophe a punishment for meddling in magic?

"Please, Tom--I didn't mean this--"

Unbuttoning his shirt, she massaged his chest, praying for a sign of life. Maybe she had been mistaken; maybe he'd only swooned. *Holy Mother of God, why did I trust a sorceress?*

A new fear grabbed her by the throat. *I've murdered my husband! I'll be hanged, and then what will become of the children?* She had to conceal the body at once. Maybe tomorrow she could invent some tale, perhaps that Tom had left at daybreak for a job in some neighboring town. Later, when he didn't return, people might assume he had been waylaid by robbers.

Though she cringed from touching him, she wrapped the corpse in her oldest sheet, the one she would have torn up for rags soon anyway. Clutching the end of the cloth, she dragged the weight across the floor. The bundle thudded and bumped with her awkward efforts. A murmur from the loft shocked her into silence.

"Mamma? What's that?"

She swallowed. "Nothing, Will. I dropped something. Go back to sleep." She stood motionless, with cramped arms and dry throat, until she was sure the boy had settled down. Then she slowly hauled her burden out the back door.

Fortunately, clouds obscured the moon and stars this night. She knew her own kitchen garden too well to need a lantern. The hens in the chicken coop rustled and clucked drowsily at her passage but didn't make enough noise to wake neighbors.

Rachel brought Tom's body to a fallow corner where the early lettuces had long since died back to a few brown leaves. With a hoe, she delved the soft soil until she'd dug a hole just deep enough to hide a man. Even that makeshift grave left her back sore and her hands blistered.

Her eyes blurred by tears, she rolled the body into the trench and covered it. Mindful of the children, little though she cared for her own life now, she raked the earth over the grave, as well as the track where she'd dragged the body from the house. *In a few days, given a summer storm or two, it should look no different from the rest of the garden.* And she knew she would have no trouble showing honest grief when her husband turned up "missing".

After putting away the tools, she washed her face and hands, crammed her soiled clothes into the bottom of the laundry basket, and slipped into bed. The firelight hurt her tear-strained eyes, so she closed them and soon fell asleep.

Some time later, she sat up, chilled by an inexplicable panic. Then the noise that had wakened her sounded again--the soft snick of the back door latch.

Who is it? Did someone see the burial, after all? She clutched the sheet to her chest, gaping at the door as it eased open.

A man's form stepped into the cottage. He closed the door behind him and lurched into the pool of light shed by the remains of the fire.

Tom! No, I must be dreaming!

Her husband straightened up, no longer swaying as if about to fall. "Rachel?" he murmured, like a man waking from a stupor.

She leaped from the bed, tangling the sheet around her as she moved, and backed against the wall. Using the sheet as a robe to cover her nakedness, she raised her free hand in the sign of the cross. "Angels and saints, protect me!"

Her husband gazed at her in a bewildered manner and held out his hand. She responded with a violent shake of her head. *Was he never dead at all? Did I bury him alive?* Her stomach heaved at that image. *No, I felt his chest, he had no heartbeat!* Was this his ghost, come back to slay her for killing him? Or was it something worse? She'd heard tales of corpses animated by demons, who stalked the earth to prey on the living.

"Rachel," he sighed. "My love, why do you flee? I only want to make you happy."

The voice sounded like his, but deeper, more musical. She took one step toward him. "Tom?"

"Sweet Rachel--my darling!" He stepped forward and sank to one knee before her, like a knight in a ballad. Clasping her hand, he kissed the palm, with a gentle flick of his tongue that made chills course along her arm.

Only then did she realize he had crossed the room with a strong, unhampered stride, with no trace of a limp. She stroked his bowed head. The hair had changed to vibrant golden curls, with a tinge of silver at the temples. Though he still looked his true age, the lines of weariness and bitterness had vanished. His voice, she realized, held a mellow richness she'd never heard before. And a scent like the sharp tang of burning leaves in autumn emanated from him.

This beauty could not spring from the Devil! The witch has kept her promise.

He leaped to his feet like a boy and wrapped his arms around her. Before she knew what he was doing, he'd swept her up and carried her to the bed. She watched him strip off his clothes. She gasped at the realization that the scars had disappeared from his chest and right leg. The hair on his body gleamed like golden wool in the firelight.

He's perfect! The potion had not brought back the husband she remembered, for neither as boy nor man had he ever looked or behaved like this. The magic had made a new man from the ruined shell of the old. *My heart's desire.*

He bent over her to unwrap the protective sheet. As each inch of cloth loosened, his lips lingered on the skin revealed there. Invisible flames licked Rachel's bosom. Her nipples perked up, and she arched her back, longing to feel his tongue on the sensitive peaks. When had he ever undressed her this way? During their courtship, he'd simply flipped up her skirts and plunged in. Every time they'd coupled in their own bed, both had already been nude.

Impatiently she wiggled free of the sheet, cast it onto the floor and opened her arms to him. He loomed over her, with his cock jutting forth like the prow of a ship. When he covered her, the thrill of the firm shaft against her thigh made her head whirl.

His mouth traveled down her chest and belly, while he murmured her name over and over. She writhed in his firm grip, struggling to bring the burning flesh between her legs into contact with his body. His tongue teased the curls on her love-mound. Suddenly a bolt of fire lanced through her. She stuffed a hand into her mouth to silence the cry that burst from her. He was lapping the bud of flesh that had ached so long for his touch. It blossomed, thickened, throbbed. "Sweet," he murmured. "Like honey." His tongue dipped into the creamy slit, then returned to the swollen nub. Wave after wave of ecstasy swept over her.

He slid up the bed, causing every inch of her skin that he brushed to twitch with near-painful pleasure. His manhood slipped into her. She felt the walls of her quim tighten, with exquisite ripples of sensation, to embrace the silk-sheathed hardness. She arched to answer his thrusts, wrapping her arms around him and sinking her teeth into his shoulder.

My perfect man! My heart's desire!

(Story originally published in *Flesh Fantastic*, ed. Amarantha Knight, Masquerade Books, 1995)

Strange Kindred

Just as twilight faded to dark, Caitlin, with the baby swaddled in a blanket and clutched to her chest, hurried into the house and bolted the front door behind her. She paused in the doorway to glance down at her five-month-old nephew. Lonn slept, oblivious to her fear. It seemed a wonder that the hammering of her heart didn't wake him.

Tiptoeing to the living room window--as if anyone lurking outside could have heard her footsteps--she twitched the curtain aside a fraction of an inch and peeked out. The street was empty, with no sign of the gleaming black, two-seater sports car she had spent the last half hour evading. *I'm turning into a scatterbrained mouse,* she chided herself. *It probably wasn't following us at all.*

Yet Caitlin had been sure she recognized the driver. Over the past week since the deaths of her sister and brother-in-law, she'd glimpsed the same man several times, in unlikely locations, beginning at the funeral itself. A lean figure with a hawkish profile and silver-white hair. He had lingered for a minute on the fringe of the graveside service, then vanished while her back was turned.

Why would a stranger stalk her? The idea made no sense. She hadn't inherited any money worth mentioning from Gwen and Niall, only the daunting responsibility for their child.

Carefully shifting the baby in her arms to keep from waking him, Caitlin headed for the makeshift nursery she had set up in her spare bedroom. She'd had to move the desk with her computer work station out of that room and jam it into a corner of the dining nook. Already her tiny house seemed crowded; what would it feel like when Lonn grew into an energetic toddler?

Tears stung her eyes as she laid him in the crib, propped on his side. He blinked his forest-green eyes, smacked his lips a few times, and subsided back to sleep.

"You're mine now," she whispered, stroking the wisps of hair that showed so dark against his creamy skin, "and I won't let anything happen to you."

She still shuddered whenever she thought of the lucky chance that had saved him. If she hadn't been babysitting for Gwen and Niall that evening a week past, Lonn, too, would have died in that freak accident.

At the moment she turned to leave the bedroom, the lights went out.

Her heart stuttered. She grabbed the doorjamb to keep from stumbling. *Power failure--no reason to panic.* Forcing herself to breathe evenly, she wondered what had knocked out the electricity. No thunderstorm tonight, just clear autumn weather.

She groped her way to the living room and glanced outside again. The street lamp on the corner still shone, as did lights in several of the neighboring houses. A shiver crept across the nape of her neck.

A shadow flitted onto the porch, attenuated but man-shaped. Caitlin pressed her hand to her mouth to stifle a scream. *Don't just stand here, go call the police, right now!* The impulse died when the silhouette sharpened into a recognizable form--but no, surely her eyes had just adjusted to the faint light from the lamppost. Tousled, dark hair framed a familiar pale, triangular face.

Niall--you're dead--

Her vision grayed with dizziness. She had to lean on the wall.

The doorbell chimed. A voice came through the barrier, low and rapid. "Caitlin, let me in."

"What--who--"

The voice was lower than her brother-in-law's, although every bit as musical despite the urgency of its tone. "Open the door! By all the lost gods, it isn't safe for me to stand out here exposed to full view."

Not Niall's ghost at all, of course. "Taran--what are you doing here--?" His twin brother, whom she had met only twice, at the wedding and Lonn's christening. He hadn't attended the funeral, and Caitlin hadn't known how to reach him.

"There's no time for this, woman." The deadbolt slid back, untouched, and the door swung open.

Backing up, Caitlin insisted to herself, *I didn't lock it securely, that's all.*

Taran stepped inside and pushed the door shut behind him, gesturing at it in a casual sidelong wave. The bolt snapped into place.

I didn't see that.

His long, cool fingers grasped her wrist. "Is my nephew well? Where is he?"

Her pulse calmed, though her forehead felt clammy in the aftermath of her near-faint. "He's fine, as much as could be expected. Come on, you can see him."

Taran gave the door a backward glance as she led him toward the bedrooms. "No wards. You're fortunate to be alive," he said with a clearly disapproving headshake.

She decided not to ask what he meant, just yet. Having him appear out of the blue like this was confusing enough.

Walking at his side, she noticed the aroma that clung to him, like newly mown grass after rain. The only previous occasion when she'd stood this close to Taran had been her sister's wedding. Caitlin had danced with him. She vividly remembered the unexpectedly strong grip of his slender hands. His graceful command of the waltz had made her, who barely knew one step from another, feel like an expert dancer. Like his brother, he wasn't much taller than Caitlin himself, yet she had felt intimidated by him. The sensation annoyed her all the more because she'd found it not quite unpleasant.

After the waltz, both needing a temporary escape from the overheated room, they had stepped outside for fresh air. They'd lost track of time listening to the noises of the night and trying to identify the insect or bird that created each sound.

They had stargazed, too, trading the names of constellations. To her surprise, she'd performed better at this exercise than he had.

He'd made an odd comment--"Your stars are different from ours."--that led Caitlin to wonder whether he lived south of the equator.

She'd barely spoken to him since--and why was she thinking of that now? She blinked away the fog that threatened to envelop her brain.

Though her eyes now absorbed more of the residual light, so that she didn't stumble in the hall, she still picked her way with caution. Taran appeared to rein in his stride, as if impatient with her for moving slowly. Could the man see in the dark, or what?

She paused at her own room to get a fat bayberry candle from a drawer and light it. In the smaller bedroom, she set the candle on the dresser and leaned over the baby, who still slept.

"Try not to wake him," she whispered. "He's been hard to settle down, ever since--" She rubbed her eyes. *This is no time for another crying session.* "I'm sure he keeps looking for his mommy and daddy. Just because he's so little doesn't mean he can't tell something is wrong."

"I'm sure you are right," Taran quietly answered, in a voice that reminded her of a spring breeze rustling through silk. His eyes, the color of moss, met hers across the crib.

She swallowed hard and looked down.

Taran reached down to brush against the baby's hand, which curled around his finger, though Lonn didn't wake. "He's in danger here," said Taran. "I've come to take him to safety."

"What are you talking about?" Caitlin barely remembered to whisper instead of yell. "Over my dead body--"

His fingertip touched her lips, making her gasp. "Hush. Let's talk about it out there."

She followed him to the living room, the candle in her tremulous hand casting wavery shadows. After setting it on the fireplace mantel, she glared at him with fists clenched at her sides. "You're not taking my nephew anywhere. Gwen's will named me his guardian, and that's that."

"He is my nephew also."

His stern calm infuriated her. "How dare you show up out of thin air? You didn't even come to your brother's funeral."

"I received word of their deaths too late."

The sadness in his eyes and voice deflated her anger. "I'm sorry. I didn't know how to get in touch with you. Sit down and explain this--danger." The image of the strange man at the cemetery leaped into her mind.

While she sat on the couch, Taran glided to the door and wove intricate gestures in the air. Caitlin thought she saw sparks flash around the lock and bolt. She shook her head; her eyes must be strained from the dim, uneven light.

"No time to set proper wards," he said as he joined her on the couch, "but that may hold off an attack long enough for me to prepare."

"Wards? What's that? Some kind of New Age stuff?"

"Not *new*." A faint smile flickered across his face. "Older than you can imagine. Caitlin, I have no time to give you the full background, and you would not believe most of the tale. There's a--man--who wants Lonn. I must take away the child tonight."

"You think I'll just let you walk out of here with my sister's baby, for a vague story like that? Think again, brother."

"He is in danger, and so are you. Tormod--"

"That's his name? The man with the platinum hair?"

"You've seen him, then?"

Caitlin nodded. "He was lurking around the graveside service."

"It's pure chance that I got here in time. Tormod plans to steal the baby, and he'll kill you if you interfere."

"But *why?*" She felt as if she had stepped off a cliff into free fall.

"As I said, you wouldn't believe me. He has already killed the child's parents, though."

"What? That's crazy. It was an accident, just a weird, senseless accident."

"Oh? Do your vehicles normally explode for no particular reason?"

His words awoke paranoid fears previously reserved for the depths of sleepless nights. *Murder. Impossible, I can't believe my sister was murdered.* "The insurance company is investigating. No, that doesn't happen to brand new cars, but they'll get to the bottom of it."

"No doubt it happened precisely because the car was new," Taran said. "Niall hadn't taken the time to place wards on it. He'd grown complacent in his life here."

"Wards, again. You're not making sense."

"I can't explain further. Nor do I have time for useless arguments. You can have a moment to pack anything the child might need and bid him farewell." He stood.

Caitlin jumped up to block his path. "You don't listen well, do you? You're not taking Lonn anywhere. Gwen and Niall trusted me to take care of him."

Taran sighed and raised a hand to finger a tendril of hair falling over her forehead. She didn't have the will to brush off his touch. "You are an obstinate, brave female. But you wouldn't have a chance against Tormod. Your sister and my brother trusted you, yes. Won't you trust me?"

For an instant she wavered, gazing into his green eyes in the undulant shadows. "How can I? I don't know a thing about you. For all I know, you're one of the bad guys."

Anger leaped into his face. His hand clutched hard on her shoulder. "How dare you suggest--harm my own blood kin--" He instantly relaxed his grip, though, and gave her a quick smile. "What am I saying? Kinship doesn't mean much, with Tormod as an example." He let out another long sigh. "Enough. As much as I would relish increasing our knowledge of each other, that will have to wait. Listen to me, Caitlin."

He smoothed the hair away from her face. "You don't want to fight me." His voice dropped to a murmur. "Don't be afraid. I'll take the child to a safe place, and all will be well. You won't need to concern yourself any further."

She found herself swaying, with her eyes fixed on his. They seemed to glitter like emeralds. Her head whirled, and a tingling warmth spread through her. What was she so worried about? Of course Taran would take care of Lonn--

About to fall, Caitlin grabbed the couch to steady herself. *What was I thinking?* She'd almost given in. Taran was trying to hypnotize her.

She vigorously shook her head and had to fight another wave of dizziness. "What do you think you're doing? I said no, and I mean it."

Taran stared at her as if she'd punched him in the jaw. "You shouldn't be able to resist the glamour. Few of your kind are that strong-minded."

"Haven't had much experience with women, have you?"

"That isn't what I meant by 'your kind'." He scowled in evident frustration. "I could take my nephew by force, but I don't want to behave like Tormod. Once more--I'll beg you, if you wish it so."

"What I want is one good reason not to call the cops."

"Blessed Lady! Very well, I'll tell you the truth." Throwing a quick glance toward the curtained window, he grabbed her by the shoulders. A volcano of words erupted from him. "Niall was the heir to an elven principality. He renounced his heritage to wed your sister. Our council agreed that the little prince--Lonn--could be brought up in your realm, provided he returned to ours when he came of age. I am regent for the babe. Tormod, a cousin of ours, tried to assassinate me and take the throne, on the grounds that the bloodline of one who'd foresworn his rightful place to mate with a mortal was unworthy to rule. Tormod was punished and exiled for that crime. He has regained his strength. Having murdered Niall and Gwenyth, he intends to take their son hostage, demanding the throne as the price of the child's life." Breathing hard, he released Caitlin. "There, woman, are you satisfied with this truth?" His eyes blazed.

She stared at him, not sure whether to laugh or scream. "You aren't joking, are you? You believe this wild story. That does it--you're nuts. Get out, right now."

"Enough of this!" He snapped his fingers. From them sprang a spark like a firefly. It expanded to a basketball-size luminous sphere and floated to the ceiling, where it hovered, shedding pearly light over the entire room.

Caitlin staggered to the couch and collapsed on it. She watched Taran shimmer, melt, and re-form, all within a couple of seconds. His face became more pronouncedly thin and sharp-featured, his fingers more slender. A faintly greenish glow emanated from his skin. And his ears were pointed.

Her chest ached from holding her breath. She gulped air and found her voice. "Niall didn't look like that."

"He wore a permanent glamour, except when he was alone with Gwenyth." Taran reached for her; she flinched, then blushed when she realized what she'd done. "One reason for wearing a human guise. Please believe that I won't harm you."

She nodded. "I have to believe it all, don't I? My brother-in-law was an elven prince. I can't imagine how Gwen managed to keep that a secret."

"Their love was strong. I often wondered how Niall could bear to give up the changeless beauty of our realm for the confinement of your world. Not only renouncing his inheritance and hiding his true nature, but accepting limits on his power. If he hadn't dwelt on this plane for so long, his magic might have protected him from Tormod."

"Our world isn't so bad," she said. "Niall always seemed so excited about everything, even thunderstorms and blizzards, like it was all new to him. Now I can see why."

"True, the mortal realm has its own beauties," Taran said, staring into her eyes.

She felt herself blush again.

His fingers traced the outline of her ear and the curve of her jaw. "I'm beginning to see that human females have a glamour of their own. After all, one charmed my brother. Your kind have hidden strengths."

Reluctantly edging away from his disturbing touch, Caitlin said, "I don't feel strong at the moment. I feel as if I'm on a sailboat in the middle of a raging sea."

"Not many of your kind could accept the things I've just revealed. You don't scream or faint in the face of danger."

She stole a glance at the window. "I guess I have to accept that part as real, too. Your cousin Tormod--"

"The traitor." Taran's voice sounded like ice.

"He's after Lonn. Oh--why doesn't the baby look--like you?"

"He is half-human, after all. As he grows, he will develop the traits of our kind." He stepped--no, glided--into the hallway. "Now, you understand why I must take him out of Tormod's reach?"

"Where? To Elfland, Faerie, whatever you call your home?" She followed Taran toward the baby's room, with the ball of light trailing overhead like a balloon on a string.

"There's no other secure refuge. I can't guarantee that I could protect him here in the mortal realm. You and Lonn have been untouched so far, only because of Tormod's unfamiliarity with this world. I'm sure it frightens and confuses him. I, at least, have visited several times. It's completely new to him. I'm sure it galls him to wear human shape and expend energy on spells to understand and speak your language."

"He must have learned to drive a car pretty quickly," said Caitlin, lowering her voice when they entered the bedroom.

"I suspect he chose a vehicle as free of metal as possible, with a body of-- what do you call it?--fiberglass. Even for someone as experienced in your ways as Niall, avoiding cold iron was difficult."

"So that legend is true." Caitlin opened dresser drawers and tossed sleepers, T-shirts, rubber pants, and other clothing items on the rocking chair. "I'd love to learn more about your people, sometime when we're not on the run from a kidnapper."

"And I would enjoy teaching you the lore of our race," Taran said. "But who knows when we might have leisure for such conversation?"

"Oh, we'll have plenty of time to talk after we get to your secure refuge. I'm coming with you."

Anger glinted in his eyes. "Why do you persist in being so obstructive? Now you're the one who has gone--as you say--nuts."

"Do you seriously expect me to send my baby to a strange place with you? Sure, I trust you now, but Lonn doesn't know who you are. He's lost both his parents. He needs me, and I'm not about to desert him."

The baby stirred, blinked at the floating light, and whimpered.

Taran waved a hand over the crib and whispered, "Rest, little one."

Lonn instantly settled into motionless sleep.

"Now he will remain undisturbed until I wake him. It's best that he not be awake for the passage through the gate, anyway."

Clutching Taran's arm, Caitlin led him across the hall into her own room, where she grabbed a suitcase and flung it onto the bed. The light followed them. "Do we have to go through a big argument over this? As you said yourself, we need to hurry."

"Brave sister, that strange place is stranger than you could imagine. Time runs differently there. How much of your life here are you ready to give up? And my kin wouldn't necessarily accept you. Most of them would regard you as the child's nursemaid or, at best, a sort of pet or plaything of mine."

Her cheeks flushed hot at the images conjured up by the word "plaything". "Then I'll just have to cope with it, won't I? Niall coped with our ways." She scooped an armful of lingerie out of a drawer.

Just as Taran opened his mouth to answer, a peal of thunder shook the house.

Caitlin gasped, her nerves quivering. "It didn't look like rain--"

"That is no natural sound."

He dashed into the living room, and she scurried after him. The front door vibrated like the skin of a drum. Around the locks danced a violet aura. Taran cast a shower of green sparks at the deadbolt. The two colors mingled in a miniature explosion. The locks burst open.

What sounded like a giant fist hammered on the door. Another starburst emanated from Taran too late to block the magic that flung the door wide. The platinum-haired man stormed in, and the door slammed behind him.

Now he looked not at all human. Caitlin stared at his pointed ears and gleaming silver eyes, at the aura that pulsed around him. He paid her no attention, though, fixing his gaze on the other elf.

"Taran. I thought I sensed you here. Just as well--destroying you now will save me trouble later." He raised his hands, palms out.

Without wasting energy on a reply, Taran lifted his hands in defense. A cone of light radiated from his fingers, fanning out and rolling like a wave toward Tormod. Already a similar wave poured from Tormod to threaten Taran.

The two waves crashed together like heavy surf on rocks. Caitlin, standing out of the way with her back to the fireplace, felt the hair on her arms bristle with electricity.

Simultaneously the two men cast fresh light-bursts. This time, when the energies clashed, she saw Taran stagger.

With a laugh like ice water, Tormod said, "You're not at full strength, cousin. You must have spent too much time in this place of rock and steel." A casual flip of his hand knocked aside a lightning bolt from Taran. "I knew your bloodline wasn't fit to rule."

Taking advantage of the enemy's instant of overconfidence, Taran threw a ball of fire. At the last second Tormod gestured to deflect it. It struck him on the shoulder, and this time he stumbled.

With a roar, his eyes blazing, Tormod launched a lightning bolt of his own. The shaft pierced Taran's hastily cast shield of green light and impaled his chest. He crumpled to the floor.

Caitlin, almost blinded by the flashes, saw him attempt a feeble wave in Tormod's direction. A glow flared briefly and flickered out. Tormod sprang like a tiger across the floor and loomed over the fallen man, with his right index finger poised like a stiletto about to stab into the heart.

Caitlin realized the touch of that finger would mean Taran's death. She blinked furiously to clear sparks and tears from her eyes. Tormod, luckily, paused to gloat. He seemed in no hurry to strike, and he didn't take any notice of Caitlin. *After all, I'm just a helpless mortal, right?*

Sidling to the fireplace, she grabbed the poker from its stand. *Cold iron.* She circled around behind Tormod. Just as the movement caught his eye and he looked up, she slammed the handle of the poker into the side of his head. She spat a curse at the weak, glancing blow. It wouldn't have done more to a human thug than make him mad.

The elf, though, collapsed in a heap on the rug. Terrified that he would get up at once, or shoot a bolt of energy at her, Caitlin hit him again, this time squarely on the forehead. A gasp from Taran stopped her from swinging a third time.

"That's enough. You've disabled him. Now, if you might put away your weapon--" Taran stared at her as if she'd changed into a werewolf and ripped out Tormod's throat.

She returned the poker to the stand and helped Taran up. Suddenly she found herself hugging him. His arms wrapped around her and sheltered her while she trembled, leaning against his shoulder. She felt his heartbeat racing in an echo of hers.

He stroked her hair. "Forgive me, but I must ask one more thing of you."

She raised her head to stare into his glowing eyes. His breath smelled like cinnamon. "Yes?"

"I have to transport Tormod into a--place--where he'll be confined, and the battle has drained my power. I need to borrow energy from you."

"Yes, anything!" Anything to keep her baby safe.

Turning her to face away from him, Taran wrapped one arm around her waist, hugged her firmly to his chest, and spread his hand over her heart. His fingers grazed the curves of her breasts. Electricity radiated from his touch, and her nipples peaked. Caitlin shivered with surges of ice and fire. Her head swam. Taran extended his other hand toward the prostrate elf. Light rippled from him. Caitlin felt as if she were dissolving, melting, while the glow enveloped Tormod like a cocoon. The luminous strands wound closer and tighter around him, until they swathed his whole body. Then he vanished.

She staggered with vertigo. Taran lifted her in his arms, and a second later Caitlin found herself in his lap on the couch. She buried her face in his shirt until she stopped shaking. His cut-grass aroma and the spicy fragrance of his breath comforted her.

"Where is Tormod?" she whispered.

"In a kind of cell, a pocket of space-time with no exit. He doesn't have enough power to break out. We should have done that to begin with, rather than simply banishing him." His hands skimmed over her body, soothing her ruffled nerves, until she wished she knew how to purr. "You needn't be afraid anymore."

"I'm not," she murmured. She felt warm and languid, as if she'd spent an hour in a hot tub. "Wish I could just stay like this all night." A blush heated her cheeks when she realized what she'd said, but she didn't move.

Soft laughter, like the ripple of a stream, came from Taran. "I share that wish, but for the moment we have other things to think of."

"That's right." She eased herself off his lap. "Now you don't have any reason to take Lonn. He can grow up here, the way Niall and Gwen wanted."

"A valid point, perhaps. Yet he does have a destiny for which to prepare. Would you deprive him of the elven side of his heritage?"

"You were all set to cut him off from his human side."

Taran gave her the first open, relaxed smile she had seen from him. "Another point to you. What do you propose, then?"

She sat up straight, determined not to be disarmed by that "glamour" he'd mentioned. "Lonn stays here until he's old enough to make his own choice. I'll allow you visitation rights, so you can teach him about his heritage. If Niall lived here full-time for a couple of years, you can certainly stand an occasional visit."

"A fair bargain." He slipped an arm around her shoulders. "There are other reasons besides my nephew's welfare that I would enjoy occasional visits. Or more than occasional." He tilted up her chin and kissed her parted lips.

Caitlin didn't resist. And it wasn't magic that made her cooperate.

(Story originally published in *Northern Hearts*, ed. Lori Paige, North Amherst, MA: Nocturnis Publications, 2000)

Nursemaid

The words of her own song jangled in Carleen's head as she fled to her car: "Little know I my bairn's father, Much less the land that he dwells in." She sank into the driver's seat, loosening bodice laces to relieve discomfort from the evening humidity, and placed her gittern on the empty passenger seat. Maybe she should have canceled her appearance as a strolling player on this last weekend of the Renaissance Faire. Only three weeks had passed, after all, a truth brought painfully to mind when a tourist had persuaded her to perform the ballad of "The Great Silkie". A song about the loss of a child was the last thing she needed. Her eyes stung with tears all over again.

Would another weekend at home have done her any more good, though? At least singing at the festival provided distraction. The emptiness of a two-bedroom condo only emphasized the emptiness within her.

She wrapped her arms around herself. Her breasts still ached and leaked sometimes. Maybe she should have accepted the lactation-suppressing drug her doctor had offered, but that would have felt like a betrayal of her baby girl.

Two months in the NICU had accomplished nothing but prolonging the pain. And she couldn't even fool herself that the ordeal would have been easier with her husband to share it. By the time of his death, they'd already stopped sharing much.

Carleen's heavy cross pendant scraped her bare arm. Now that she no longer needed to stay in character as a pilgrim to the shrine at Canterbury, entertaining her fellow travelers, she took off the necklace and tucked it into her purse. It would only get in her way while she drove. Enough brooding, she decided; she wanted to get on the road before twilight faded to dark. With a last glance at the multicolored tents of the Faire and the turrets of the Victorian mansion visible above the trees beyond, she inserted the key in the ignition.

A man knocked on her window. Carleen jumped, then hastily pushed down the "lock" button. She thought better of her momentary panic when she peered at him through the glass.

He stood less than five feet tall, stocky and slightly hunched, and his outfit of russet and green proclaimed him a member of the festival cast. She rolled down the window and stared into his bearded face. The word "dwarf" popped into her head, despite the contemporary preference for "little person". This man was clearly costumed as a not-quite-human creature from Scandinavian or German myth.

"Mistress O'Brien?" He spoke in character, even though the Faire had closed down for the season a few minutes earlier.

"Yeah, what can I do for you?"

"My name is Roark. I serve Lord Elwin. He wishes to see you."

This guy certainly took his role to heart. "Lord" Elwin did suit the owner of the mansion and the surrounding acres, Carleen had to admit. For five years he had allowed the local Renaissance Faire to use his land, and he always made one personal appearance per weekend, dressed in brocade and velvet to fit his assumed title. Not this time, though, come to think of it.

"He could have seen me during the day, while I was performing. I'm really tired and need to get home--"

The "dwarf" grabbed the edge of the window. "He's recovering from an injury. Please, Mistress, it's most important."

For a second Carleen felt tempted. Every year, she had enjoyed the spectacle of Padriac Elwin's golden hair and flawless features, not to mention his long, muscular legs in Tudor-style hose. Even a year ago, recently married, she had felt free to savor the view. The Faire's patron had paused to listen to one of her ballads and complimented her on it.

But this year she had no interest in handsome men. "Sorry, Mr.--Master Roark. If you can't tell me what this is about, I'll pass."

His voice dropped to a growl. "Then I have no choice."

Carleen saw a flash of silver in his hand. Something pierced her neck like a hornet's sting. Her vision went gray, then black.

Her head swam, and her stomach lurched. When she opened her eyes, the world swayed. Gradually she realized the little man was carrying her. He must be stronger than his height revealed. Kicking and squirming didn't loosen his grip.

His voice rumbled in her ear. "Please don't, Mistress O'Brien. Lord Elwin doesn't want you harmed."

"How nice of him. Put me down."

To her surprise, Roark set her on her feet. She had to cling to him until her head stopped spinning. They stood in a hall at the top of a curved staircase. Carleen turned to bolt toward the stairs.

Roark grabbed her arm. "Lord Elwin wants to see you at once."

Rather than waste energy in useless struggle, she let him lead her to a half-open door. For a second the air shimmered, and a rainbow of light rippled in front of her eyes. *What did he do, drug me?* When her vision cleared, she found herself in a combination bedchamber and sitting room, large enough to hold three of the master bedroom in her condo. A single lamp shone beside the double bed. A milky aroma pervaded the air. A noise assaulted her ears. At first she couldn't place the sound, which resembled the wail of a Siamese cat.

She identified it a second before her eyes lit on the bassinet near the far wall. Her nipples tingled. She hugged herself, feeling damp patches on her bodice. Squeezing her eyes shut to stop the tears, she silently cursed Elwin.

The man himself, golden-haired, clothed in a silver-gray robe, stood beside the bassinet. He jounced the crying baby in his arms.

"Don't be so rough," she began, then chopped off the sentence. *I will not get involved!*

Elwin's eyes fixed on her. "It's about time. Yes, she'll do very well."

Carleen broke out of Roark's loose hold and lunged toward her host. "Look here, Mr. Elwin, what gives you the right--"

He shifted the baby to the crook of one arm, wincing as if the movement pained him, and held up a hand to interrupt her. "Just Elwin, please. Won't you sit down, Carleen?"

She checked her headlong charge. "I won't be here that long." It didn't seem important that he called her by her first name, compared with the indignity of being delivered like a parcel.

The baby's clenched hand collided with his chest. He grabbed the waving arm and tucked it back into the blanket. "You have no choice about staying, I'm afraid. But I don't want to make it unpleasant for you." His voice quivered with strain.

She folded her arms and scowled at him, wishing he looked ugly or at least menacing, instead of like a sculpture of a Greek god. "You really think you can get away with kidnapping? People will start missing me soon." She stared straight at him to avoid looking at the bundle he held.

"No, they won't. You are a widow living alone." His brilliantly green eyes scanned her, raising a blush on her cheeks. "Recently you have isolated yourself from your friends. No one will be surprised at not hearing from you."

All true, she realized with a sudden constriction in her chest. "My gig at the Ren Faire--"

"Come, now, Carleen, I know this was the last day of the festival. They won't search for you, either."

"How do you know all that?"

"Roark made inquiries."

Her shoulders sagged. "Then you also know I'm not rich. Not a candidate for ransom." As if a man living in a house like this would need money. Also, he didn't look like a rapist or serial killer, but, then, most of the successful ones didn't, did they? "What are you after?"

"I have a desperate need only you can fill." Elwin closed his eyes, frowning as if his head ached. He shoved the screaming baby at her. "Here."

Her arms automatically curved around the infant to support its head. "What do you think you're doing?" She tried to give the child back to Elwin, who retreated a couple of steps. An expression that resembled panic flitted across his face.

"You can't just dump your baby on me like this!" Against her will, her gaze dropped to the little face, contorted and red from wailing. It turned toward her breast. She stiffened.

"Yes, you're exactly what I need." Elwin darted around her and followed Roark into the hall. Before she thought to make a dash for it, the door slammed.

The baby's cry grew louder. She ran to the door and grabbed the knob. It wouldn't turn. She rattled it, banging on the panel with her free hand. "Elwin!

Roark! Damn it, let me out!" Finally, her throat hoarse, she leaned on the door with tears streaming down her face. "Damn you, don't make me do this," she whispered.

She trudged across the room and lowered herself into a rocking chair. The baby momentarily stopped screaming. The eyes, not blue like the average newborn's but green like Elwin's, gazed up at Carleen. Was this why Roark had snatched her, to take care of Elwin's child? The man could certainly afford a nanny. The whole episode made no sense, but she couldn't focus on puzzling it out. The baby squirmed and nuzzled her breast, mewling.

She'd never actually nursed her own daughter, only pumped to fill the bottles she delivered to the hospital. Nevertheless, her body knew what to do. Her fingers shook while unlacing the bodice. Freeing a nipple, she hugged the baby close. Its gums fastened on her, provoking a gasp of pain that merged into harsh sobs. She closed her eyes and rocked. After a while the rhythmic tug of the baby's mouth, the sucking noises, the sway of the rocker, and the warm flow of milk soothed her. By the time both breasts were drained, her tears had stopped. She felt calmer than she had since her endless night of premature labor.

The peace couldn't last, she knew. This baby didn't belong to her. It belonged to a man crazy enough to kidnap a strange woman instead of calling a temp agency. She settled the baby in the bassinet and fumbled for a diaper. The child turned out to be a boy, who waved his limbs in the aimless manner of a newborn. Though he looked plumper than Carleen's premature daughter, he couldn't be more than a couple of weeks old. She lowered a tentative hand into the bassinet. As if hypnotized, she reached toward the baby's flailing arm. The tiny fist closed around her finger in the typical reflex grip. Within a minute, though, he relaxed into sleep.

In the attached bathroom she washed her face, then drank a couple of glasses of water. Refreshed, she marched to the bedroom door. The knob turned freely. She brushed aside the uneasiness roused by this discovery. It must have been stuck before, or she had panicked and twisted it the wrong way.

To her surprise, the corridor seemed different. It stretched a disorienting length in both directions. Something must have gone wrong with her vision, because she couldn't focus on the far ends of the hall. And what had happened to the stairs?

She turned in what she thought was the right direction and paced off fifty steps, then a hundred. She passed one closed door after another without noticing any variation in them, the floral-papered walls, or the carpeted floor. Lightheaded with growing fear, she reversed direction and broke into a run.

Nothing changed. The same corridor lined with doors stretched on and on. Finally, panting, she paused to lean against the wall. Up ahead, she sighted an open door. Walking toward it, she thought it looked like the entrance to the baby's room. Seconds later, she confirmed that impression.

How did I get here? Too confused and anxious to explore any farther, she dragged herself into the room and fell onto the double bed.

Carleen woke to a tentative knock.

Roark stood in the doorway. "I've brought your things from your carriage." He dropped her purse, overnight bag, and gittern on the sofa.

She sat up, rubbing her eyes, and glared at him. "How long do you think you can keep me here? Show me the way out right now, and I won't press charges."

Roark shook his head. "Lord Elwin and the child need you, Mistress."

On top of everything else, he was still playing a Ren Faire role. She barely suppressed a shriek of exasperation. "He can hire a nurse, like anybody else. What will you maniacs do when somebody notices my car?"

"No one will. It's well hidden on the grounds."

Without further speech, Roark carried the diaper pail into the hall and replaced it with an empty one.

This procedure momentarily distracted her from her worries. She had trouble imagining Roark doing laundry, though the house didn't seem to hold any other servants. Maybe Elwin used a diaper service.

When the dwarf had gone, Carleen took a shower and fed the baby again before changing into jeans and a T-shirt. If she had to remain a captive for the present, she was glad she didn't have to wear the Tudor costume. Searching the dresser and walk-in closet, she found smocks, sleepers, and other baby clothes, as well as a collection of loose gowns that might fit her if she got sick of jeans. As for underwear, she would have to wash it by hand. *What am I thinking? I won't stay here long enough to worry about that.*

Roark brought her food in the morning, fruit and whole-grain bread with a carafe of milk. He paid no attention to Carleen's demands for release. After another exploration of the hall, which brought her back to the same room, she spent most of the day rocking the baby and reading a Sir Walter Scott novel she discovered in a bookcase full of age-mellowed volumes beside the bed. In the afternoon she got restless enough to try the windows. She was unsurprised that they wouldn't budge.

Just as she gave up, to gaze with yearning at the sun-dappled trees that surrounded the house, Roark arrived.

"Mistress O'Brien, Lord Elwin wishes to see you."

"Oh, why don't you drop that fake medieval dialogue?"

With no change of expression, the little man said, "And bring your gittern, if you will."

Carleen's first impulse was to refuse, but she thought better of it. Why antagonize her captor unnecessarily? Maybe if she acted resigned to her fate, these two weirdos would drop their guard. She removed the gittern, a small, stringed instrument resembling a guitar, from its leather case and followed Roark a few doors down the hall. Again she saw no sign of the elusive staircase.

Roark knocked on a door, opened it, and ushered her into a study or parlor, furnished with upholstered chairs, a coffee table, a matching desk of polished wood, and bookshelves. Elwin, dressed in the same silver-gray robe, reclined on a couch.

"You have my profound gratitude for your care of my son," he said as soon as Roark left them alone.

This greeting threw Carleen's anger off track. "Well, I couldn't ignore a helpless baby, could I?" She sat on a chair near Elwin and struggled to gather her thoughts. "But that's no excuse for what you've done. Why don't you just hire a nanny?"

"My child was starving. I needed a woman who could nourish him, not a mere caretaker." He didn't sound deranged; in fact, his earnest tone threatened to undermine Carleen's indignation at his behavior. The musical resonance of his voice, reverberating through her nerves, didn't help.

She steeled herself against the reaction. "Ever heard of formula?"

"I tried that. He couldn't live on it. He has been wasting away for a fortnight."

She felt a stab of pain between her breasts. "You know, some organizations supply mother's milk for bottle feeding--"

Elwin shook his head. "No, Carleen, I needed you."

He was a lunatic after all, even though the most ravishing one she'd ever met. His marble-pale skin only enhanced his attractiveness.

"How could you possibly know I was--qualified?" She blushed when his eyes roamed over her bosom.

"As I told you, Roark made inquiries among your friends at the festival. I know your own babe died only three weeks ago. And I remembered your singing from past years. You render the old ballads with rare insight."

"Spare me the flattery," she said, trying to fend off the image of her tiny girl in the isolette hooked up to monitors and IVs.

"Roark described to me how you sang the tale of the Great Silkie yesterday. You understand what it means to lose a child."

"That's just folklore. A half-human child being carried off by his father who's a shapeshifting seal doesn't have anything to do with a real baby dying." Her voice rasped with pent-up tears. She swallowed them, determined not to cry in front of this man.

"Nevertheless, I know I can depend on you to care about my son."

"Of course I care!" She caught herself clenching her fists on her lap. "That doesn't give you the right to drag me in here and use me for a brood mare. I'm not some animal who can't tell the difference when you replace one baby with another."

"I never assumed that." His long, slender fingers touched hers, sending an unexpected shiver up her arm. "I had you brought here because I was desperate."

"What happened to the baby's mother?"

"She died in the same accident that injured me."

Though Carleen wondered what kind of injury Elwin had suffered, she resisted the impulse to ask. The thought sprang to mind that they had something in common, the deaths of their mates. She suppressed it. If she wanted to avoid emotional entrapment, she'd better not learn too much about his situation. So she only said, "I'm sorry about your wife."

"We were not married." His lips tightened as if in pain. "Would you do me a small favor?"

"You've got some nerve asking."

"My head aches," he said. "I would be most grateful if you would sing for me."

"Grateful enough to let me go?"

A smile fleeted across his face. "You are perfectly welcome to leave if you can."

That remark offered an opening for her to ask about the endless hallway, but she didn't want to give him the satisfaction of refusing to answer. Instead she picked up the gittern and played the ballad of "Tam Lin", the young man held captive by the Queen of Elfland until the mother of his unborn child risked her life to free him. Elwin closed his eyes, the lines of strain disappearing from his face.

She thought he'd fallen asleep until he murmured a "thank you" and drowsily looked up at her. "Tell me, Carleen, what happened to your husband?"

"Why do you ask?"

"Only my dismay at finding so kind and lovely a woman alone in the world."

He sounded as if he really meant it. "Jake died in a plane crash on the way back from a business trip," she said. "He never even knew I was pregnant. I was going to tell him when he got home. We hadn't been married long, and we weren't planning a baby right away. It just happened."

Elwin nodded. "I can well understand that."

"I thought it might bring us together. Silly, isn't it? A man won't change from a workaholic into a homebody just because he becomes a father. I can't imagine why I didn't realize what Jake was like before we got married. Fooling myself, I guess." She hadn't even taken his name; maybe on some level she'd known they weren't suited.

"Susceptibility to illusion is a trait most human beings share. Don't allow that to increase the burden of your grief." He leaned over to clasp her hand.

Waves of warmth rippled through her. "I don't have any parents or other close relatives living. I think I jumped at the first chance to build a family of my own."

"Yes, family is of the greatest importance."

Why was she revealing herself to him? She pulled her hand free and hardened her heart against his sympathy. "You can't expect me to forget my baby because of yours, no matter how sweet he is. I'm not a sheep or a cat. The sooner you let me go, the less trouble you'll be in." She stood up, clutching the gittern.

"It isn't forever," he said. "I only want you to stay here as long as Rian needs you."

So that was the baby's name. "I'll take care of Rian while I'm here, but the minute I can escape, I'm gone. So you better start working on a contingency plan."

"I can reward you well," he said in a cooler tone.

"I don't need your money!" Jake's insurance had paid off the condo and left her enough funds that she could live without working for a couple of years, if she chose to squander the money that way. She'd set up automatic debits to pay for utilities and other recurring expenses. It occurred to her that if she had a job or paid her bills by check, at least somebody would miss her. Until this moment she hadn't fully realized how isolated she had become in the past few months. "I don't need a thing from you except my freedom."

"That is impossible." Elwin lay back and closed his eyes again.

She stormed into the hall and had no trouble finding "her" quarters, although when she peered up and down the corridor, its far ends faded into mist. Again she wondered whether Elwin and Roark had drugged her. Surely a man who cared about his infant son wouldn't risk drugs in the breast milk. On the other hand, this guy's elevator didn't go all the way to the penthouse. Maybe as soon as she found a phone, she should report him to the child welfare office.

Rian stirred and whimpered when she entered the room. She carried him to the rocking chair. Already he recognized her enough to stop crying when she picked him up. She stroked his wispy growth of pale golden hair. He responded with a flicker of a smile before nuzzling her chest. Carleen knew some people attributed these early smiles to "gas", but she'd never believed that theory.

He's not mine, she reminded herself. *I can't get attached to him.*

As soon as he'd been fed, washed, changed, and put back to sleep, she made another circuit of the windows. They were all stuck shut. Maybe she could pry up one of them. True, she didn't have the acrobatic talent for climbing down the outside wall, but making a rope ladder of sheets might work. Anyway, she had to get a window open first. She'd already searched the room in vain for useful tools. Her overnight bag held only clothes and toiletries. The idea of spraying Roark in the face with aerosol deodorant had crossed her mind, but what good would that do? She couldn't find the stairs, much less the front door. The gittern case contained nothing but the instrument and spare strings. She smiled wryly at the image of strangling her captors with gittern strings.

She tried to remember whether she had anything in her purse sturdy enough to unstick a window. Sitting on the bed, she reached in the purse and pulled out one useless object after another--wallet, day planner, pen, tissues-- *Why don't I carry a screwdriver?*

Her fingers closed on the cross she'd worn with her Ren Faire costume. The air shimmered. A spicy aroma perfumed the atmosphere.

She blinked away a rainbow-hued mist. The room looked different; for a few seconds she wasn't sure how. Then she realized that the late afternoon sun revealed a layer of dust over every surface except the furniture she had used. Cobwebs festooned the corners of the ceiling. When she scanned the room, she noticed that the bookcase now seemed only half-full.

She rubbed her eyes. The gray coating of dust didn't evaporate. Slowly standing up, she hung the cross pendant around her neck. With a fantastic idea gnawing at her brain, she forced herself to walk over to the bassinet.

The baby opened yellow-green eyes shaped like a cat's. His golden hair was now white, and his skin had the faintest greenish tinge. No longer plump, he mewed like a kitten and waved stick-thin arms at her. And he had pointed ears.

Carleen backed away, her hands pressed to her face. She drew long, shuddering breaths, choking down the scream that threatened to burst from her. *Oh, God, no, this can't be real, let me wake up!*

She dashed into the bathroom and splashed water on her face until the threat of hysterics waned. Drying herself, she noticed that the modern fixtures had been replaced by a claw-footed tub with a rudimentary shower ring, a pedestal sink, and a toilet with an overhead tank. Still fighting to keep a grip on herself, she reflected that she should be grateful Elwin had outfitted the bedroom with real furniture.

Okay, I don't have to panic. I've read enough folk tales and ballads to know what's going on here. Assuming she wasn't crazy and hallucinating, Elwin was a faerie lord. In the legends, elven folk often kidnapped human females to nurse their infants. The cross had broken the glamour that kept her from recognizing the baby's true nature.

Confusion gave way to anger. *Well, "Lord" Elwin, I'm not about to let you get away with this!* Carleen stalked into the bedroom and stared at Rian. Though strange-looking, he wasn't ugly. In fact, he had an exotic beauty. His catlike eyes met hers, and he whimpered.

He was still an innocent baby, after all. She couldn't blame him for his father's behavior. She picked him up and cuddled him until he dozed off. "I'm sorry, sweetie, it's not your fault, but I can't stay. I have to get out of here." She laid him in the bassinet and brushed away tears.

Grabbing her things, she hurried into the hall. Immediately she saw the top of the stairs less than twenty feet away. She rushed downstairs and had no trouble finding the foyer. The front door had a simple bolt that didn't need a key to open. After she'd drawn it, though, the doorknob wouldn't turn. She instantly thought of the "stuck" knob on her bedroom door the previous night. Probably every exit in the house, doors and windows alike, had a locking spell. If Elwin could cast illusions, why not other kinds of magic?

She ran upstairs, dumped her bags in the hall, and barged into Elwin's room. Vines crept over the shelves and entwined the furniture legs. Bell-shaped flowers that glowed pale green and rustled in an unfelt breeze peeked out of every corner. A heady fragrance permeated the air.

Elwin glanced up from a book. "To what do I owe this visit?"

"You know damn well what! I want you to remove the spell that's keeping the front door locked."

"So you've seen through the glamour." His eyes alighted on the cross. Feline eyes, to match the pointed ears and elongated fingers.

She leaned over him and shoved the pendant into his face. "Let me go right now."

With a soft chuckle, he pushed aside her hand. "Do you expect me to burst into flames? What do you think I am, a vampire from one of your moving pictures? This symbol makes you immune to the glamour because it represents the new order that banished us from your world. It doesn't hurt me."

Carleen plopped into a chair, breathing hard. "Why? At least tell me that. Is Rian's mother really dead?"

With a deep sigh, he nodded. "I suppose it can't do any harm to tell you the full truth now. She was human."

"Did she know about you?"

"No, and that led to her death." He sat up and leaned toward Carleen, gazing into her eyes. "I came here almost seven years ago, as you measure time. My father is the chief of our clan. I quarreled with him. He disapproved of my forays into the human world."

"Why?"

Again he emitted that soft, musical laughter. "Too dangerous for his heir. Too much cold iron in your modern culture. When I defied him once too often, he punished me with exile. If I liked mortals so much, let me dwell among them for seven years, he proclaimed."

"If he thought our world was too dangerous, that wasn't a very logical punishment."

"Our kind tend to be passionate and impulsive. Not to mention obstinate. If I had fallen victim to some fatal accident, he would have hidden his grief and appointed one of my cousins heir in my place."

"That sounds so cold."

His lips curled in a humorless smile. "Oh, I could have cut short my exile at any time by groveling to my father. I didn't want to return that badly. I regarded my stay here as a sort of adventure--a very human notion, I must confess. Even if some of those dangers are real."

"But they haven't gotten you. Not so far, anyway."

"Not lethal ones, at least. I did lapse into a very brief liaison with a human female. She had no idea of my true nature. We spent only a few nights together and parted kindly enough. I expected no consequences."

"The baby," said Carleen.

"Yes. The woman sent me a message two days after Rian's birth, demanding that I come to her. Roark drove me into the city."

"If you're allergic to iron and steel, the way the tales say, how can you ride in a car?"

He grimaced. "It is uncomfortable, but I manage. I can't drive one, of course. Fortunately Roark, being of dwarven blood, can use the tools and machines of your technology."

"So you met Rian's mother, and she gave you the baby."

"That's understating the matter. Away from the magical refuge I've created, in the midst of a large city, there was no spell on her vision to disguise what she'd given birth to. She raged at me for impregnating her with a 'monster' and demanded that I take the child off her hands."

Carleen's heart constricted. She couldn't imagine rejecting her own baby, no matter how it looked. "Then you took custody of him. What happened to the mother?"

"We argued. She refused my one request, that she nourish him for a mere few weeks. She tried to force me to leave, and we continued our quarrel outside. When I tried to restrain her and make her listen, she ran from me. A truck speeding around the corner struck and killed her. Attempting to save her, I was also hit."

His bleak tone chilled Carleen. "By iron and steel. That's why you aren't well yet."

"Yes."

"Then you took Rian."

"After casting a glamour on everyone who had seen me, to make them forget I'd been there."

"You just left her?"

He gave Carleen's hand a brief, painful squeeze. "Don't you see? I couldn't do anything for a dead woman, and if I hadn't erased all evidence of my visit,

I might have lost my son. Three hundred years ago, such a babe would have been cast out to die, as an imp or a changeling. Today, he would survive as a freak, an experimental subject for your science." He leaned back, holding her gaze with his own. "As I told you, I haven't been able to feed him. Even human milk from a bottle, if I could obtain it, wouldn't be enough. Our infants need to be nursed."

"I understand why you're desperate." The image of her own baby flashed into her head once more. "But that still doesn't mean you can just take over my life indefinitely." Another aspect of the traditional tales sprang to mind. "Oh, my God, I've eaten your food. How long have I been here? Am I going to leave and find out a century has passed?"

Elwin smiled. "Hardly. You aren't inside the Hollow Hills. This house lies entirely within your world."

"Thank Heaven for that, anyway."

"Carleen, my dear, I'm not asking for your life or any large portion of it. My exile ends in less than a month. When my father's retainers come for me, I'll take Rian to our own realm, where I can find an elven woman to nurse him. All I ask is that you stay until then."

She no longer felt afraid of Elwin. She ached in sympathy with his need. What made her reluctant was the fear of becoming daily more attached to Rian. She didn't know whether she could endure the loss of another baby.

Yet how could she risk letting him starve?

She drew a deep breath. "All right, I'll stay that long."

Though she figured she was now immune to Elwin's glamour, Carleen continued to wear the cross, just in case. The first thing she did was to rip a few of the shabbier garments in the closet into rags and dust the bedroom. She demanded an assortment of cleaning supplies from Roark to scrub the bathroom and sweep cobwebs from the ceiling. "I can imagine two men, even if they aren't human, living this way, but with a baby in the house you can't just cover up dirt with illusion," she griped to the dwarf. "Come to think of it, if you can lock doors with a spell, why didn't you make the dust go poof?"

"That would be a waste of magic," he grumbled back at her. "In the mortal realm we have limited access to the power."

"Then you should have done it by hand. I ought to make you help. Who do you think I am, Snow White?" Actually, though, she welcomed the occupation.

Once she'd finished the cleaning project, she had no duties other than caring for the baby, who slept longer than most fully human infants of that age. Boredom drove her to spend more time with Elwin, despite her better judgment. Getting attached to Rian would be bad enough. The last thing she needed was to become attracted to his father, a trap she could easily fall into.

Elwin appreciated her songs, unlike Jake, who had merely tolerated her "hobby". The elf-lord taught her new ballads in English, Old French, and Gaelic, and once he sang to her in a language she'd never heard before. It sounded more like birdsong than words. She didn't need to be told that it wasn't a human tongue at all.

They traded riddle songs: "How can there be a cherry without a stone? How can there be a chicken without a bone?" Not surprisingly, Elwin knew the answers to all the verses. His kind had probably invented them.

"In these songs," she mentioned once, "the mysterious stranger quizzing the maiden always turns out to be either an elf-knight or the Devil himself."

Elwin arched his golden eyebrows. "Do I strike you as diabolical?"

"No, but I think you're dangerous." She stifled a gasp at her own boldness. He only laughed.

Each night before Rian's bedtime, she carried him in to visit his father. Elwin conjured dancing lights to entertain the baby. When Rian's hands tangled in the threads of multicolored light and scattered them, Elwin laughed aloud. His eyes glowed with an unguarded delight that made Carleen's heart stutter.

She slipped into the habit of dining with him each evening while the baby slept. The food varied little from meal to meal. She got used to living on fruits, juices, bread, and no animal products except milk and cheese. Elwin also served a sparkling wine that reminded her of honeysuckle and evaporated on the tongue so fast she barely had time to swallow it.

One night she asked him about his home.

"How can I describe the realm within the Hollow Hills so that you can visualize it? Your world roils with constant turmoil of birth, death, greed, loss, decay. Ours is free of that noise and confusion."

"But some human beings have visited it, according to the legends."

"A few stumble in by accident. Others are stolen away by elven lovers or choose that fate of their own desire."

She recalled the ballads. "Like Tam Lin and Thomas the Rhymer."

"Most of them eventually leave, though."

"And the stories say they're never the same again."

He twirled a wineglass and gazed beyond her into the darkness outside the window. "It leaves its mark upon them, yes. Sometimes I have trouble remembering, myself. The memories fade into mist when I try to invoke them. Imagine a world of unchanging spring, with foliage perpetually green and flowers always in bloom. A world without cold or rain, unless conjured into temporary existence for sport. I remember one interlude with a landscape of white and silver, the tree branches like wind chimes of crystal..."

"Sounds like Camelot," she said. "Or California without earthquakes and flash floods."

With a half-smile, he shifted his eyes to focus on her. "Better than that. Matter in our world is not the heavy, dull mass you wrestle with in your struggle for survival. Every element around us responds to our wishes--even our whims."

"What if your whims happen to clash with somebody else's?"

"If we cannot compromise, there's always the option of a duel." He chuckled at her dismayed stare. "With magic, most often, not weapons. We have rivalries, true, but they seldom become lethal. The worst outcome is usually exile, like mine, if the victor has the power to enforce it."

"You miss your home." After the anguish of the past year, Carleen thought a refuge of changeless tranquility sounded attractive.

"At times--its beauty, and the pleasure of shaping that beauty by magic. Yet I confess your world has its charms. Its chaos and the obstinacy of its matter can be stimulating. Strangely seductive, in fact. Some of my kin might charge me with becoming too fond of your Earth, unfit to rule our homeland."

"Are you looking forward to ruling it?"

He shrugged. "It is my duty, I suppose. And I will enjoy having my full powers restored. If inheriting my father's reign is the price of that--" Leaning over to refill his glass from the wine carafe, he winced.

"You still hurt from getting hit by the car, don't you?"

He nodded. "I almost feel I deserve it, for failing to save the life of my child's mother. My kindred would be aghast at such a weak, human-like attitude."

Far from being "aghast", Carleen felt warmer toward him, discovering that he could experience guilt. "Can't you do anything to heal yourself?"

"Not here. Once I've returned home, the pain will soon vanish." His feline eyes mesmerized her. He moved closer and ran his fingers over her hair and down the curve of her jaw. A shiver rippled through her. "Your music helps."

"I wish I could do more." She couldn't manage more than a whisper. Her breath seemed trapped in her throat.

"You could," he whispered. "This."

He eased nearer, until she could smell the fragrance of the strange wine he'd drunk. His mouth brushed hers. Her lips parted with an involuntary sigh. The flicker of his tongue sent electricity dancing along her nerves. When she closed her eyes, a prismatic glow sparked behind the lids. She felt his hand swirling over her back and down her spine in ever-deepening spirals.

I swore I wouldn't let this happen! She broke away from his kiss and sat upright in her chair, gulping ragged breaths.

"I would not force myself on any woman," he said, his own breathing shallow and uneven. "But I would like to share this pleasure with you."

"Sorry, I think of it as more than pleasure."

"So do I, my dear. Pleasure is only the beginning."

She smoothed her disheveled hair back from her face. "Another thing the legends claim--immortals can win human souls by taking mortal lovers. There's no truth in that, is there?"

He shook his head. "I know nothing of souls. But one thing we can gain from a human mate's embrace. We draw energy, vitality, through our inborn magic. No harm comes to the mortal, only a fleeting lethargy."

"And I'll bet elven lovemaking is unforgettable." She put an edge on the comment to fight off the unwanted images flooding her mind.

"Some of your people have said so."

"What a line!" She stood up. "That's my cue to leave. See you tomorrow." She hurried back to her room before she could weaken.

She flung herself across the bed, her head spinning. She would be crazy to let Elwin seduce her. According to every legend she'd heard, the Faerie folk had no capacity for love in the human sense. Immortal and ageless, they pursued their erotic adventures in a spirit of cold frivolity. Look at the way

Elwin had dallied with Rian's mother and promptly forgotten her. And even if Carleen could delude herself that he felt true affection for her, she couldn't become entangled with him. His exile ended within a couple of weeks.

She inhaled a deep breath of the spicy fragrance in the air and rubbed moisture from her eyes. So soon after recovering from the loss of her husband, how could she make herself vulnerable to another male?

Too late, my shell has already cracked. She sensed the frost around her heart melting even as she fought to deny the reaction. So what if she and Elwin could share only a few nights? Because Jake had disappointed her in marriage and then abandoned her by dying, did that mean she should never risk herself with another man? And whether or not he was human was beside the point. If she avoided his touch from this moment on, his departure would hurt just as much. Why deny herself and him a passionate interlude?

I'm just a pet to him, a plaything, she warned herself, already stripping off her clothes, draping herself in a sheer nightgown, brushing her hair. This entire adventure meant no more than a dream, anyway. Since she recognized their time together as a temporary enchantment, all the better that they shared only sensual delight. That awareness should make parting less painful. And she had no fear of pregnancy, since breastfeeding had kept her periods from resuming yet.

After checking to make sure the baby was soundly asleep, she tiptoed down the hall to Elwin's door, which was now shut. She tapped on it. When he called her name, she stepped inside. A soft glow from no visible source provided the only illumination. He stood in the doorway between the study and the bedchamber. Motionless, he waited for her next move.

"Elwin--" Her chest felt tight. She had to force out the words. "If we make love, will you be healed?"

"Yes."

"I'd like to believe that's not all you want from me."

"It is not."

He stretched out a hand. She allowed his tapering fingers to capture hers in a cool clasp. He guided her to his bed, overarched by a canopy of vines. A cloud of fragrance, like cinnamon and cloves, hovered in the air.

While she knelt on the bed, he lit a pair of bayberry candles without touching them, by a casual nod. She watched him strip off his robe. Naked, he ran his fingers through her unbound hair and swept it back to kiss her neck and shoulders. She trembled as he pulled the gown over her head and tossed it aside.

Quivering with self-consciousness, she wrapped her arms around her swollen breasts and wished she could hide the stretch marks on her abdomen, too. Except where shadowed by greenish bruises, his slim, hairless body looked flawless in the undulating candlelight. He gently unfolded her arms and nibbled his way to each nipple, licking droplets of milk. An ache spread downward, forcing a moan from her. He raised his head to kiss her parted lips, and she tasted honeysuckle.

Her hands roamed over his smooth, pale skin, while he explored her body, spiraling lower, inch by inch, until her barriers melted away. His amber-flecked green eyes sparkled, making her dizzy with the effort to focus on them. She let her own eyes drift shut. She forgot all fear as he plunged into her like ice and flame.

Again and again she melted, re-formed, and shattered under his touch. Each time he arched in ecstasy above her, he cried aloud in that alien, musical language. Finally he carried her back to her own bed.

When Elwin visited Carleen and Rian the next day, he displayed a vitality she'd never seen in him before. The bruises had vanished. And his ease of movement confirmed that their embraces had healed his wound. She saw no point in avoiding a repeat performance, now that her serenity was damaged beyond repair. Whenever the baby slept, Elwin seduced her with fierce intensity, and she offered no resistance. He had none of the limitations of a human male. She stopped trying to count the times he ravished her.

Between these encounters, they shared meals and songs. One night he invited her up to the roof, encircled by a railing and outfitted with a telescope, to show her the stars. Earth's constellations, he said, held endless fascination for him, since only a dome of pearly mist arched over his homeland. "Iridescent pastels by day," he said, "and deep blue by night, with thousands of fireflies dancing in the trees. But no sun, moon, or stars. I shall miss some things about your world."

Otherwise, he never spoke of his imminent departure until the final night. He came to her room dressed in a tunic and breeches with a green cloak, similar to the outfits he used to wear when visiting the festival. He lifted the baby to his shoulder and said, "My punishment is finished. My father's emissaries will arrive soon."

Carleen felt tears gather in her eyes. She practically snatched Rian away from Elwin. The baby wailed, and she had to calm him. Hugging him to her breast, she kissed the top of his head and struggled not to cry. "I know he has to go where he belongs, but--" She choked on the words. She preferred not to acknowledge, even to herself, how much she grieved to see Elwin go, too.

He drew her into an embrace, the baby between them. "My dear, you needn't be separated from him. I would suffer from losing you, just as he would. Why not come with us?"

"What?" She squirmed out of his arms and passed the child to him. "You can't mean that?"

"Why not? You know the tales of your people who have lived within the Hollow Hills."

"Yes, and we've discussed the way those people never really fitted in." She batted away his hand when he reached for her. "I'd be a toy for you, a pet at most. What would happen when you got tired of me?"

"Carleen, beloved, I never--"

"And don't try to snow me with vows of eternal love. We're two different species. How could I stand getting old and withered while you stay young forever?"

"It isn't that way." His gleaming eyes pierced her. "As long as you remained within my realm, you would share that eternal youth."

"And I can just imagine what your father, the chief, would think about you bringing me home like a stray puppy." She turned away from his mesmerizing gaze, afraid he might enchant her against her better judgment. "Not a chance. We had our fun. It's over." She didn't want to admit the allure of that invitation, to retreat to a place of perfect, changeless serenity. False serenity, she reminded herself. Not designed for short-lived human beings.

"Consider this." He grasped her shoulders and forced her to meet his eyes. "In our world, your grief will dissolve like a snowflake in the sea. You will forget all your sorrows."

"I don't want to forget them. They're part of me."

"A very human answer." He released her. "As you wish." Did she actually hear pain in his voice? "You will stay and bid me farewell, won't you?"

"Sure." Did the word sound as brittle to him as it did to her? "Say, what about Roark?"

"He remains here as caretaker of the house. He was born in this world. His kind, as I mentioned, are better suited to Earth than mine. Now, I don't have much time. Will you climb to the roof with me?"

The sun had just set when they emerged at the top of the mansion. "I thought you'd have to go somewhere else to cross over into your world--a portal of some kind."

He shook his head, draping a fold of his cloak around the baby as a shield against the wind. "Human travelers need gates, places where the wall between worlds grows thin. We can cross at will. Except for the banished ones like myself, of course."

They watched the sky in silence for a while, his free hand clasping hers. At moonrise, electricity crackled around them. Carleen felt her hair lifted as if by an intangible wind, and the same energy made Elwin's hair bristle like a lion's mane.

The space in front of them sparkled and coalesced into a pair of tall figures in silver robes. One of them raked his eyes over Carleen. Her knees quivered, but she nerved herself to stare back at him.

The other visitor spoke to Elwin in their own tongue.

"Show courtesy to my companion!" Elwin snapped. "Speak her language."

"Very well." The other elf's voice sounded as cold as crystal bells. "We have come to escort you to your father's court. Give the babe to his mortal nurse."

"What are you saying?"

"Surely you didn't expect to bring a half-breed whelp with you into the Hollow Hills."

Elwin handed Rian to Carleen and faced the two emissaries with his arms folded. *No!* she silently cried. *You can't give him up!*

With her pulse pounding in her ears, she almost didn't hear Elwin's next words: "That objection has no merit. Our population has dwindled over the centuries. We need every child."

"Not this child."

Something like a growl rumbled in Elwin's chest. "Countless half-elven children, as well as human changelings, have grown up in my father's realm."

"Only as pets. Our lord would never accept a child of impure blood as his future heir."

"Impure!" Elwin's eyes flashed. "You speak of my son."

"Be reasonable," said the elf who hadn't spoken before. "Your sire waits to welcome you back into his court. Scores of women among the ranks of our nobility would delight in helping you forget this escapade. You can beget full-blood children upon them."

"I do not desire any of them." Elwin glanced at Carleen, who stared back at him with the baby cradled in her arms. "If those are your terms, you'll have to return without me."

"Impossible. You are the heir. Our clan needs you."

"I have several cousins who would leap at the chance to assume that role. Let my father choose one of them."

"Once you've passed the boundary between worlds, your memories of exile will fade to a fleeting dream. You'll soon forget you ever cared for any inhabitant of this world."

"I don't want to forget." He turned toward Carleen, his eyes glowing.

The first emissary shook his head in evident disgust. "You'd give up your birthright for a half-human brat."

"I won't leave my son." Elwin reached for Carleen's hand. "Or my beloved."

"You're mad. Compared to our lifespan, she'll survive no longer than a butterfly. And she'll decay with age before that."

"Enough. Carry the message to my father." He pulled Carleen close and enfolded her in his cloak.

The two visitors vanished in a coruscation of multicolored light.

Her head spinning, Carleen clung to him, with the baby snuggled between them. "It could happen," she said. "You might regret it. You said it yourself, our world constantly changes."

"Yes." His lips brushed the top of her head. "I look forward to the adventure."

The Crystal Tesseract

Julian was the last person Danielle expected to see at her aunt's funeral.

Yet the moment she stepped out of the limousine and glanced up, blinking away tears in the late afternoon San Diego sun, she felt his eyes upon her. And when she found the source of the intent gaze that seemed to burn her skin like the sun itself, she knew him instantly.

A vivid memory blindsided her--their last day together before the disaster. A tall, skinny boy of fifteen and herself, a shy twelve-year-old. They rambled over the desert hills, as they'd done so many times before...

She remembered Julian lending her his jacket to put on over her sweatshirt when the wind picked up and made her shiver. "I don't get cold much," he'd said. "I just wear it because Mom bugs me."

She had to scurry to keep up with his long legs. The spiky leaves of ice plants crunched under their feet...

Danielle rubbed her eyes to erase the image. Where had he been for the past fifteen years? After the breakup of the Order of the Crystal Tesseract, the children in the group had been dispersed to foster homes or relatives. Aunt Lisa had firmly discouraged any discussion of that catastrophic period. "You have a normal life now," she always said. "Forget about all that crazy cult stuff."

Spasmodically clutching her purse in her left hand, Danielle picked her way across the lawn to the folding chairs at the graveside. Out of the corner of her eye she glimpsed Julian taking a seat in the back of the little group. Her heartbeat quickened. She forced her mind away from him and struggled to concentrate on the brief graveside ritual. A few minutes later, she let out a sigh of relief at the final "Amen" and hurriedly made her farewells. As the other mourners dispersed, Danielle paused in her walk back to the funeral home's limo. Julian stood in her path.

She felt dizzy for a second. *Too much sun in my eyes, that's all it is. He can't have any effect on me, not after all this time.*

"Julian. Thanks for coming. I didn't notice you in the church."

"I wasn't there. Wasn't sure I'd be welcome. But I had to see you." His rich baritone made her stomach flutter.

He took off his sunglasses. When his eyes captured hers, she discovered her memory hadn't embellished their strange, brilliant green. She had to look upward to meet them. He'd been tall at fifteen; now he towered well over six feet. He'd made her feel tiny then, and even more so now.

He clasped her hand. The cool, dry grip made her pulse accelerate again. She expected him to offer a conventional condolence like the ones she'd been fielding for several days. Instead, he said softly, "Were you happy with your aunt?"

"As much as could be expected, I guess. She was good to me." Tears prickled her eyes.

"Then I'm sorry for your loss."

He wore black trousers with a white shirt and forest green tie, but no jacket. His black hair curled almost to his collar. Still gazing into her eyes, he stroked her palm with his thumb, rousing a shiver that ran up her arm and all the way down her spine. Of course it was too much to hope that growing up would have made him any less devastating.

With his free hand, he swept a tendril of her short, wavy hair back from her forehead. "You still have those same blue eyes and flaming red hair," he said. "But you've lost the freckles."

She managed a shaky laugh. "Well, I hope so. In high school I kept wishing I could wear a bag over my head."

"I thought they were cute."

Danielle forced her eyes away from his face. Suddenly aware of the funeral home driver waiting for her by the limo, she freed her hand. "I have to go now, Julian."

"Just like that?" His low voice created a bubble of intimacy around the two of them. "Please, Danielle, let me see you again."

"That would be--yes, why don't you come over for dinner?" She felt breathless, almost lightheaded. "And there's another thing--my aunt left me something--strange--something connected with the Order. Maybe you--"

Julian started; then his face went blank. "Of course. Anything to help." The flat tone jarred against the caressing voice he'd used a moment before.

After setting a time and giving him the address, she watched over her shoulder as he strode to his car. *Why did I do that?* Because he was the only person available who had shared her bizarre childhood?

On the way back to the mortuary to pick up her car, then during the drive to her condo in La Jolla, Danielle couldn't stop thinking of Julian and the commune. Even there, he'd been the strange one, the one other children's parents warned them against.

The mystery of his parentage had certainly contributed. In a community whose official doctrine dismissed marriage as an archaic instrument of superstitious oppression, Danielle's parents, legally bound by "that piece of paper", had been the exception. Still, most of the children either had two parents on the premises or at least knew the identity of the absent one. Nobody knew who Julian's father was. His mother, one of the founders of the Order, never volunteered any information. If Julian himself had any idea, he didn't discuss it.

"That boy gives me the creeps," Danielle's mother had said more than once. "Those weird eyes of his, like a cat's. And he acts way too grown up for his age. Not to mention how thin he is. Are you sure he doesn't have some kind of chronic disease?"

But Danielle hadn't been able to stay away from him, and he'd tolerated her crush. No matter if he thought of her as a kid sister. They shared long conversations, alleviating the loneliness she felt in this peculiar place where her parents had brought her after selling the house, quitting their jobs, and pulling her out of second grade. All of the other children except Julian were too young for her to consider as playmates.

Over the five years she'd spent in the commune, almost forgetting what "normal life" in the outside world was like, she had grown from a child to a twelve-year-old adolescent. The gap between Julian and her began to close. Her hero-worship changed to something sweetly painful that she didn't dare express. About that time, she had stopped telling everybody she was going to marry Julian when they grew up.

Danielle recalled the final hours before the disastrous night that had destroyed the Order and robbed her of her parents. A bright December afternoon, the day of the winter solstice and Yule Festival...

At the top of a ridge the two of them looked back at the scattered buildings of the Order's property, a failed dude ranch the founders had bought at a bargain price.

"What do you think you'll do when you grow up?" she asked. "I mean, we can't stay here the rest of our lives, can we?"

He waved at the cluster of houses in the distance, gray with sun-faded paint. "I hope not--what a dump!" His mocking smile faded. "The Archons are training me for a special destiny."

"What?" she breathed.

He flopped down on his back, hands behind his head. "Can't tell you. It's a secret."

"Julian--!"

"Okay, I admit it--I don't know. Mom and the Archons just drop hints. Cryptic crap, as bad as the rituals in the temple."

"Oh, like the stars coming right and all," Danielle said, disappointed. "Same old thing." She sat beside him, arms clasped around her knees.

He pulled a clump of ice plants out of the ground and tossed it several yards. "They have to let me go to college. They can't home-school a physics degree or whatever. And then--"

The noise of barking interrupted him.

Glancing up, Danielle saw three dogs loping in their direction, a German shepherd, a collie, and a medium-size, floppy-eared mutt. They all looked skinny, with matted fur. They trotted closer, snuffling and panting.

She extended a tentative hand to the nearest, the shepherd. "Good dog?" He sniffed her fingers. She caught a whiff of his rotten-meat breath. The mutt's lips curled back in a half-growl, half-whine.

Julian slowly stood up. "These aren't nice doggies." He reached for her hand.

At the sound of his voice, the mongrel shifted to a full-throated snarl. The other two dogs joined in.

Clasping Danielle's hand, Julian tugged her to her feet. "Let's get out of here," he said. "Walking. No sudden moves."

Hanging onto each other, they backed up. The dogs kept pace, stiff-legged, growling. Danielle noticed a gleam of drool on the shepherd's muzzle.

"Do you think they've got rabies?" she whispered.

"Don't have to. Feral dogs in packs just like to attack pets--and people."

The dogs closed in. Julian let go of her. "Run!" He gave her a gentle shove and darted between her and the animals.

She spared a second to glance over her shoulder. He made a sideways shooing motion, his eyes on the dogs. She broke into a stumbling run over the rough ground.

Her heart pounded against her ribs, her lungs aching. She tripped. Pain shot through her right ankle, and she tumbled onto the hard-packed earth.

At the same instant, a neon-green flash burst on her sight. She rolled over to look back at Julian and the beasts.

A swirling green haze filled her vision. Through it, as if through several feet of murky water, she saw the wavering shapes of the dogs. And something else, something that hurt her eyes to stare at. Something with lashing tentacles, too many to count, that twined around the mongrel and hauled it into the air.

An insectile buzz assaulted her ears. Her head felt ready to burst. She glimpsed the other two dogs turning tail and fleeing. Emitting sparks of multicolored light, the writhing mass of tendrils vanished with its captive.

Danielle blacked out.

It must have been only seconds later that she regained awareness, wrapped in a warm, tight embrace. Julian knelt on the ground behind her, holding her against his chest. She felt his chin resting on the top of her head.

"It's okay," he whispered. "They're gone."

She turned enough to raise her head and look up at him. To her astonishment, he planted a light kiss on her lips. She drew in a gasping breath. For a second she imagined that his eyes glowed. Another burst of light flooded her vision. She felt as if she'd plunged into a pool of warm liquid that slid over her skin like satin. Her head reeled; she lost contact with the earth, weightless.

A second later, her sight cleared, and the ground felt firm under her again. *What was that? Did I hit my head on a rock? No, I'm okay--and this is just Julian.*

When he bent toward her again, she closed her eyes. His lips brushed hers more deliberately, making her skin prickle with a sudden shiver. His open hand clasped her firmly around the waist. Her recently-budded breasts tingled.

He must have sensed her tightening with uneasiness, for he relaxed his hold. She scrambled to her feet, wincing at the pain in her ankle.

"Oh, you must've sprained it." He sank to one knee beside her and wrapped his fingers around the ankle. A surge of heat soaked into the muscle and bone. After he let go, she no longer felt stabs of pain when she put weight on the foot. She still hobbled with weakness, though.

They spoke very little while he helped her limp home to get it bandaged...

Danielle snapped back to the present as she pulled into the parking space at her townhouse condo. *I imagined that glowing thing, or fabricated the image later. It couldn't have been real. Julian couldn't actually summon up demons, could he?* Nor could he have healed her sprained ankle with a touch. It must not have been twisted as badly as she'd thought.

That night, December 21st, the cataclysm had occurred. No wonder her memories of everything surrounding that event were distorted.

After the whole community's Yule celebration, with the usual invocations of the Unspeakable Name, the One Who Sleeps, the Lurker at the Threshold, and the Opener of the Way, the full initiates--most of the adults--had gathered in the temple, a converted barn, for a more esoteric midnight ritual. Unusual excitement had hung in the air that year, an atmosphere fraught with whispered conversations abruptly cut off when children entered the room. Julian had suspected some extraordinary ceremony in the works, but even he didn't know what it might be.

A few minutes after midnight, an earthquake had shaken the area in a five-mile radius around the commune, and the temple had disintegrated in an explosion whose cause had never been explained. Three adults had escaped the devastation--two occupied with watching the children, and a third in bed with the flu. Neither Danielle's parents nor Julian's mother had been among them.

Danielle flashed on a memory of the moment when she had awakened to find her bed vibrating under her. One of the two children who shared her room, a little girl only four years old, had started wailing. A slender Hispanic woman they all called Aunt Elena rushed in to comfort them. A second tremor struck, and Aunt Elena tripped onto the four-year-old's bed. Through the window facing the temple, Danielle saw a bright flare, like a sheet of rainbow-hued lightning covering the sky. A noise like a sonic boom had burst on her ears...

She realized her hands were shaking. She squeezed the steering wheel until her knuckles whitened, then forced herself to let go and draw long, deep breaths. *That was fifteen years ago. It's all over.*

San Diego County police officers had picked up the children a few hours later, and within a week Danielle had moved into her unmarried aunt's home in nearby Chula Vista. Since then, she hadn't seen or heard of anyone else from the Order.

In the house, she shed her black dress and changed into shorts and a soft, faded U.C. San Diego T-shirt. Pouring a glass of iced tea, she considered heating up one of the casseroles left by Aunt Lisa's friends. Her stomach knotted at the thought.

At her desk in the extra bedroom she used as an office, sipping the tea, Danielle ran her fingers over the floral carving of the small cedar-wood box she'd found in a locked drawer in her aunt's room. She hadn't looked inside the box yet. Once again she unfolded the letter that had directed her to this find, the handwritten letter Aunt Lisa had composed in the hospital during her last few days of life:

Dear Danielle,

In my top dresser drawer you'll find a certain object that your mother gave me the week before the accident. The key to the box is in my jewelry chest. You may not want to open it, but that should be your own decision.

It's an artifact belonging to the cult. Just before their deaths, your parents were planning to leave the commune. Your mother told me she'd discovered that their rituals weren't just "fooling around", as she put it. The elders of the group actually planned to summon beings from "Outside" to lay waste to the world. She stole this object, she said, to make it impossible for the plan to work.

It sounded like nonsense to me then and still does. But--

I tried to destroy the thing. A sledgehammer didn't even dent it. After that mysterious explosion, it seemed safest to keep the object secured. I didn't dare just throw it away. I locked it in a box and haven't looked at it since.

If any cult members are still alive elsewhere, they must not have suspected what happened to the artifact, because nobody has ever come looking for it.

I'm sorry to leave you this burden. The best advice I can give is for you to do what I've done. Lock it up in a safe place and forget about it. After all this time, I doubt you're in any danger from mad cultists trying to recover their property.

I've done my best with you, and I pray you've been happy. Remember that I love you.

Danielle folded the letter, blinking away fresh tears. Lock it up and forget about it? Curiosity about her parents wouldn't let her follow that advice, however sound it might be. And now that Julian had reappeared, she felt she'd received an omen. Surely they were meant to open the box together.

She idly traced the roses carved on the lid. She imagined a tingle in her fingertips, like static electricity. Forgetting the tea, she sat staring out the window at the palm tree in the side yard, her mind drifting.

The doorbell wrenched her out of the reverie. *How long have I been woolgathering?* The palm tree cast a long shadow in the sinking sun. She felt a flutter under her diaphragm as she headed for the front door. Abruptly she wished she had put on something more flattering than shorts and T-shirt.

She opened the door, holding her tea glass in one hand. Julian took off his sunglasses and stared down at her.

"Danielle. I'm so glad you asked me over. I'd hoped we could talk."

He'd changed into a lime-green T-shirt that highlighted the color of his eyes. Still thin for his height, he projected an impression of wiry strength rather than frailty. The knitted shirt clung to well-defined chest muscles.

She swallowed a lump in her throat. "Come in, Julian."

Stepping inside, he held up a bottle of Chardonnay. "I don't know if this is a suitable offering for a death in the family, but I wanted to bring something."

She thanked him, wishing she could think of a remark that wouldn't sound conventional and banal. "It's fine. I was really surprised to see you. How did you find out?"

"I still read the San Diego paper, and I noticed the obituary. Since I live in the Los Angeles area, I took a couple of days off so I could run down here."

Los Angeles--so close, all this time! She suppressed the impulse to ask why he'd never called or written. *I'm twenty-seven now, not a teenybopper with a giant crush.*

Pausing in the middle of the living room, she said, "Let's start dinner. We can drink the wine with the meal." Abruptly she realized her stomach felt hollow.

He followed her into the kitchen. Rummaging in the refrigerator turned up a tuna casserole, which Danielle popped into the microwave. Julian sat on a high stool next to the central island, while she tossed together a salad on the butcher-block counter.

"What happened to you after--you know?" she asked. "Did you have any family to go to?"

"No, the County stuck me in a foster home for three years, until I turned eighteen."

She poured him a glass of iced tea and refilled her own. "I'm sorry. That must've been rough."

"It was hardly *Oliver Twist*," he said with a dry laugh. "They didn't beat or starve me. They were okay, I guess. I didn't expect to be smothered with love anyhow, so we got along all right. Just sort of left each other alone."

Danielle shook her head. "I can't imagine what I would've done without Aunt Lisa. She was a lot older than Mom--too old to be saddled with a flaky pre-teenager--but she really tried."

"Flaky? You?" he said with a half-smile.

"I woke up screaming every night for weeks. I had a terrible time adjusting to school--didn't start to make friends for more than a year. She must have gotten awfully tired of my sulking. And then there was church." Danielle couldn't suppress a giggle at the thought of all the Sundays Aunt Lisa had dragged her out of bed and made her dress up. "I finally had a change of heart and decided to get baptized and confirmed on my own initiative. After I figured out that praying to the Opener of the Way to resurrect my parents wasn't accomplishing a thing."

Julian's eyebrows arched. "I should think not. Have you forgotten all the Order's teachings? The Ancient Ones don't have the slightest interest in the welfare of individuals. They just want us to help them break through into this world and take over."

"Yeah, I know." She applied a knife to a green pepper with vigorous chopping strokes. "And they'll scour the earth clean of all organic life except a handful of people they'll keep as cattle. And their worshipers, who'll get to rule over the common herd--if we're very, very faithful." She shook her head again. "What a crazy religion! I can't believe our folks did that to us."

He shrugged. "Makes sense if you accept the basic premise. After all, if the Ancient Ones' victory is written in the stars, who wouldn't want to be on the winning side?" He sipped his tea. "So what are you doing nowadays?"

"Working as a research librarian at U.C. San Diego. How about you?"

"When the system cut me loose at eighteen, I went to U.C.L.A. I didn't have any relatives, but I had a nice comfortable trust fund, so that was no problem."

She handed him a corkscrew to open the wine. "So did you major in quantum physics the way you planned?"

"I started out that way, then switched to computers. More marketable. I'm a programmer with a company in Pasadena."

They moved to the redwood table in the dining nook, where he poured the Chardonnay while she dished up salad and casserole.

After eating in silence for several minutes, Julian said, "At the cemetery you mentioned your aunt left you something--what is it?"

"No clue. She kept it in a box, which I haven't opened yet. Her note said it was something my mother stole from the Order."

He froze with fork in hand. "And your aunt didn't even give a hint what it was?"

Danielle shook her head. "Must have been something important. Mom and Dad were planning to leave the cult when they--before the accident." She swallowed some wine to dislodge the lump in her throat. "I can't help wondering why they would bother to take some artifact first. That would only give the Archons a reason to hunt them down."

"Are you worried about that?" Julian spoke in a low, strangled tone.

"After all this time? Not really. Like Aunt Lisa implied in her note, if they wanted to get it back, they would've tried by now. If there were any members of the Order left."

"You don't think there are?"

The question surprised her. "They were all killed in the explosion, right? All but three."

"How do you know our temple was the only one?" Instead of following up this suggestion, he changed the subject. "Why did you want me to help you check out this--artifact?"

Blushing, she glanced down at her plate. "It does seem a little strange, I guess, when we haven't seen each other in so long. But I was never close to any of the other kids. Just you."

"I know." His voice softened as he reached across the table to lightly clasp her hand. "Me, too--you."

"But you were so much older and more mature. I had that incredible crush on you, and you must've thought of me as a kid sister."

He squeezed her hand, and her pulse sped up. "At first. Not by the time they separated us. I'd have been blind not to notice you were growing up."

She felt her cheeks growing hotter. *Must be the wine.* "Julian--if you felt that way, why didn't you ever write? I gave you Aunt Lisa's address before the cops picked us up, didn't I?"

His eyes widened. "I did write--three times. When you didn't answer, I figured you just wanted to forget everything about that part of your life."

A rush of anger constricted her chest. "I guess that's what Aunt Lisa thought, too. Why else would she have made sure I never got those letters?"

"You would've answered, then?"

"You know I would! Missing you was part of what I cried over every night."

His face flushed, too, and he let go of her hand. They finished the meal in silence. Outside, darkness had fallen.

When they moved to the living room with coffee, he said, "Well, what about that--thing? I admit I'm curious."

Leaving her cup on the coffee table, Danielle went to get the box and its key from the office. "Her note said she locked it in this jewelry case and never looked at it again."

Julian ran his palm over the lid like someone stroking a cat. "Well, let's see it." He sounded short of breath.

She inserted the key in the lock. It stuck, and she had to jiggle it several times to make it catch. With a click, the lid cracked open. Danielle raised it, surprised to find herself holding her breath.

Inside the box she saw a crystalline, three-dimensional *something*. When she picked it up, it scintillated with prismatic colors. Lightweight as plastic, it seemed to comprise a nest of interlocking cubes, each face about two inches square. Turning the object over in her hands, she tried to trace the connections. Her eyes got lost in a visual maze, as the cubes interpenetrated each other.

"Like a Mobius strip," she breathed. "So the name of the Order wasn't just symbolic. There really is a Crystal Tesseract."

"And it's not lost after all," Julian whispered. He kept his gaze fixed on the thing, like a knight-errant adoring the Grail. He reached for the crystal and touched it with one fingertip.

A flash of light burst forth. An electric shock sizzled in Danielle's palm. Blinded, she dropped the crystal with a yelp of pain. She felt Julian clutch her arm.

Within seconds her sight came back. She blinked at the sparks floating before her eyes. Why did the room look so dark?

"The electricity cut off," she murmured.

She saw Julian's shadowed form bend over to pick up the crystal with slow deliberation and place it in the box, which he set on the coffee table. Her eyes still dazzled with afterimages, she groped her way into the kitchen for a candle and matches.

When she returned to the living room with a fat bayberry candle that shed a flickering light, she found Julian motionless on the couch, his fists clenched on his thighs. He stared up at her.

She carefully lowered herself to the couch, placing the candle in the center of the table. "Your eyes glow," she whispered. They did, yellow-green like a cat's in a shadowed corner.

He bowed his head and shaded his brow with one hand. "I didn't mean for you to see. I didn't know that would happen when I touched it."

"You can't tell me this power failure is just a coincidence." She heard a tremor in her voice. Though she couldn't feel afraid of Julian himself, this situation, and the thing in the box, scared her.

"No, I wouldn't try to tell you that."

"Look at me, Julian." She tugged on his hand. "I won't freak. Not right away, anyhow. I just want to *know*."

He raised his head to stare at her. "The crystal was supposed to be used in that Yule ritual. They went ahead without it, which is probably what caused the explosion."

"How could you know that?"

"The Order has a branch in L.A. They've kept in touch with me all along." His luminous eyes riveted hers with disconcerting intensity. "I told you, back then, that I had a special destiny."

"Then you're still--one of them?" *Maybe I should be afraid of him after all.*

"Sort of. They think I am, anyway. Now that I've found you again, I'm not so sure. You see, the Crystal Tesseract is my heritage, to be claimed when I turned thirty. And I had my thirtieth birthday a few days ago."

"So when you touched the tesseract--"

"It--knows me. I was bonded to it as an infant. I was born to wield it."

"Wield it *how?*" She heard her voice turn shrill with rising fear.

"You know what the purpose of the Order was. To bring back the Ancient Ones when the stars turned right. The stars come right in the month of my thirtieth birthday. It was planned that way, so I can draw upon my full power and open the Gate."

"This is crazy--" She inched away from him, her fingers curled, nails biting into her palms. "You can't believe all that stuff about higher dimensions, monster deities from the spaces between the stars."

"If I'm crazy," he said, "how do you explain this?" A wave of his hand indicated the darkened house.

Danielle tiptoed to the window and peeked out between the curtains. No lights as far as she could see. "Oh, God. I do not believe this." She pressed the back of her hand to her mouth, stifling a whimper that threatened to well up into hysterics.

She took several deep breaths and returned to the couch. "Okay." Seated at the opposite end from Julian, she wrung her hands in her lap. "Okay. The Crystal Tesseract is real, and it has supernatural powers. And you're supposed to use it to invoke the Ancient Ones. Now what?"

"Now the Archons in Los Angeles will be expecting me to bring it back to the temple there, so we can perform the ritual."

"Wait a minute. You must have known all along that I had the crystal. How?"

"On the night of my birthday I could feel it--drawing me like a magnet. It was sheer coincidence that I read about your aunt's death around the same time. If she hadn't died, I would have invented some other excuse to visit you."

Tears blurred Danielle's eyes. "All that talk about old times and caring about me was fake. You just wanted this thing."

"No, Danielle!" He slid closer and reached for her hand. She didn't have the will to snatch it away. "I do care. I've thought about you since then, so many times. Until I felt the call, I didn't have any idea your family had the crystal all this time."

She rubbed her eyes with the back of her free hand. "If you really cared, why didn't you contact me?"

"Because I thought you hadn't answered my letters and didn't want a thing to do with me. Because even if you did--" He briefly shifted his eyes away from hers. "I didn't want you exposed to any danger."

"What danger? Getting zapped? Look, I have to admit the crystal has-- unusual properties. I don't have to believe in demonic entities from Outside lurking to pounce on us and eat us alive."

"Don't try to turn it into a joke." He ran his palm over her hair, making her shiver. "It's real."

Danielle shook her head. "I don't want to listen to this crap. If you still believe it, the cult has finally driven you nuts."

He opened his mouth to speak again. The front door burst open.

Julian let go of her hand and sprang to his feet. A slim, blond man in jeans and a T-shirt barged into the room. He carried a pistol.

"What the hell are you doing here?" Julian growled.

"What do you think? Hand over the crystal, and I won't have to shoot your girlfriend."

Danielle slowly stood up, her eyes darting between the two men.

Julian shifted position to stand between her and the intruder. "Wrong answer, Dean. If you don't want to get hurt, leave."

The man smirked. "Say what? You hiding an Uzi in your back pocket?"

"The Archons decided not to trust me, is that it? They sent you for backup?"

"To follow you, just in case. You've been here hours longer than you should've needed to grab that thing. So I'm taking it."

"The hell you are! It's mine, and I decide--not some errand boy!"

If he was trying to provoke the man into a rash misstep, he failed. The gunman just shrugged. "Hey, man, I'm following orders, that's all. Like you're supposed to be."

After a quick glance over his shoulder at Danielle, Julian glided closer to the other man. "I'm wondering how the Archons hope to use the crystal without my cooperation. Or didn't they mention that part?"

"Not my problem." The man leveled the pistol and started to edge around Julian. "Enough talk. Get out of my way, and I'll take it and go."

"Too bad the Archons didn't explain a few other things." Julian reached for the man, who dodged him and fired the gun.

Danielle's ears rang. She screamed. Violet light blossomed in the center of the room. At its core, she saw Julian's figure melt into an undulating, ameboid blur. A whiplike appendage lashed out and flung the pistol to the floor. The man screeched and grabbed his wrist. His hand hung limp, as if broken.

The coruscating cloud enveloped him. He vanished.

Danielle screamed again, her hand pressed to her mouth. The pulse pounded in her temples; her head reeled.

The light contracted upon itself, congealed into a multi-tentacled shape with countless gleaming eyes. One tentacle plucked the gun from the floor and flicked it into the air. It, too, disappeared.

With her knees shaking, Danielle sank onto the couch. The thing dissolved into Julian's human form--human except for the pair of eyes that glowed green.

For a few seconds he gazed steadily at her. Then his legs crumpled.

She staggered to him, breaking his fall just in time to keep him from banging into the table where the candle flickered. Dragging him to his feet, she helped him to the couch and made him lie down. Only then did she notice the dark, wet patch on his shirt.

"He shot you--"

Julian nodded, squeezing his eyes shut.

"You have to get to a doctor, get the bullet out."

"No," he whispered. "Bullet's gone. When I--changed--it went away."

"Away? Where?" She heard her voice rising to a shriek. She breathed deeply, struggling against hysterics.

"Don't know. Wherever Dean and his gun went."

"Never mind that." She stepped to the phone, focusing on what she did understand. "You need help. I'm calling 911."

He said nothing while she listened to the silence and jiggled the receiver cradle.

"It's out, too," she said. "I'll have to drive you to the emergency room."

"No need. Really. Besides, your car probably won't work either. Come here." He lifted one hand, let it fall to his side.

She knelt on the floor beside his head. He groped for her. She draped his arm around her shoulders, not sure why she didn't run screaming into the night. *This is Julian, and he saved my life.*

He drew her close. His eyes searched hers in silent appeal. She bent to press her lips to his. They felt chilled and tasted like the scent of the air before a thunderstorm. He explored her mouth with tiny nibbles, coaxing her lips apart. His mouth warmed under hers, and his tongue teased her.

She closed her eyes, moaning aloud. A flood of heat surged over her. Neon lightning sparked behind her eyelids.

She broke out of his embrace and rocked back on her heels, lightheaded. Julian sat up. With unexpected strength, he half-lifted her onto the couch.

Her vision blacked out for a few seconds. When her eyes focused, she saw Julian sitting beside her, felt him arranging throw pillows to prop her up.

"Are you all right?" he said in a firm, resonant voice. "I'm sorry I had to do that."

"Do what?" she said, her voice slurred.

"Borrow energy from you to heal myself. Remember your twisted ankle that time? But this wasn't quite so easy. And it's always harder to do it to myself than somebody else."

"Borrowed energy," she repeated. That was the least crazy thing she'd heard or seen within the past hour.

"You'll recover soon. Don't worry."

"What happened to that man? What did you do to him?"

"I told you, I don't really know," Julian said. "When I--reach out--that way, things or people just--go somewhere. I don't know where."

She shuddered. "Is he dead?"

"If not now, probably soon. I suspect where they end up isn't a real place at all, just some kind of interdimensional void. Same with that dog that attacked you when we were kids."

She swallowed against a surge of nausea. Gray spots swarmed before her eyes. Leaning her head on her knees, she felt Julian get up and heard him walk toward the kitchen.

A minute later, he sat down again and forced a glass of ice water into her hands. She gulped half of it before speaking.

"Julian, what in heaven's name does this mean? What are you?" Based on the mythology they'd learned in childhood, the answer seemed obvious. "One of those creatures from the outer abyss, disguised as human?"

"Only half right," he said. "My mother was human. She offered herself as the vessel for a child who would grow up to bridge the gap between dimensions. Me."

"That's why you were bonded to the crystal."

"Which won't work without me, at least that's what I was taught. I can't imagine what the Archons had in mind, unless they planned to kidnap you as a hostage for my cooperation."

"To open the Gate for the Ancient Ones to invade our dimensional plane. If that isn't complete and utter craziness." She fortified herself with another sip of water, wishing for a dose of something stronger. "So you claim you're not on board with that anymore?"

"The Archons clearly had their doubts." He put his arm around her. She stiffened momentarily, then leaned into the embrace. "I've had thirty years to get used to this world the way it is, get attached to it. Trouble with my being half human, from their viewpoint, is that I have human weaknesses. Such as love."

"How can you talk about love when you haven't seen me in fifteen years?"

His lips grazed her hair. "Doesn't mean I ever forgot. And meeting you now, seeing Dean threaten your life--well, you saw how I chose. The Ancient Ones can forge themselves another tool. Whenever the stars align properly again, which could be a hell of a long time, from what I've studied."

Her eyes wandered to the coffee table. "What about the crystal tesseract?"

"Too dangerous to keep lying around," he said. "As soon as the electricity comes back on, your car's battery should fix itself too. We'll get rid of the thing tomorrow."

"Yeah, how? Aunt Lisa tried--"

"It can't be destroyed, but living water should neutralize it, make it dormant. I'll weight down the box, chain and padlock it, and drop it in the Pacific."

"You make it sound so simple." She clasped his hand. "What if the cult comes after you again?"

"For what? Without the crystal? I doubt any of them want to end up like Dean. We're free to start over, together. If you want to try."

He's not human! a voice in the back of her mind cried. *Never mind,* a stronger voice countered. *One step at a time. He's still Julian.*

He'd never forgotten her, after all. He'd risked his life to protect her.

She tilted her face up to his. "Yes, I want."

(Story originally published in *Romance And Beyond*, Vol. 2, No. 4, Winter 1999-2000)

Storm of Passion

Another peal of thunder crashed. Seconds later, the lightning flashed in Jane's aching eyes.

With cramped fingers, she gripped the wheel to stop her compact car from sliding on the wet pavement. Between the downpour and the lightning flashes, she could barely see where the road ended and the surrounding woods began.

A figure appeared in the glare of the headlights. A man, standing directly in front of the car. Instead of jumping aside, he raised his hand in what looked like a casual wave.

Dark hair, white shirt, dark splotches on his face and shirt--

Blood--

Slamming on the brakes, Jane wrenched the wheel to the right.

The tires shrieked, and the car slammed into a tree. The crash jerked her forward against the shoulder belt.

Gulping shuddery breaths, she bowed her head on the steering wheel until her heart slowed. With a muttered "Damn," she yanked open the door and stood up on wobbly legs.

"Hey, are you all right?" She could barely hear her own voice over the wind.

Circling around the rear of the car, she slipped in a patch of mud. With another curse, she pulled herself up and used the vehicle as a prop to support her until she had a clear view of the road.

Lightning flashed again. The empty road.

Jane blinked and rubbed her eyes. A few more cautious steps brought her to the passenger side, where she took a flashlight out of the glove compartment. She scanned the roadway and the woods on either side. Nobody.

"Great--first the idiot scares me halfway to a heart attack and makes me crash, then he takes off."

She trained the flashlight on the hood. The front bumper was crumpled, and suspicious-looking fluids trickled underneath.

"Anybody here? Where are you, dammit?"

Getting no answer, she snatched the key from the ignition, then pulled her oversize purse out of the front seat and slung the strap over her shoulder.

"It was a dark and stormy night," she muttered as she started walking.

With luck, she would find help around the next curve.

"There've got to be houses not too far away," she said, still talking aloud to ward off the dark. "This isn't a howling wilderness. That guy must've popped up from somewhere." Unless his car had broken down, too.

The flashlight enabled her to stay on the pavement and out of the mud but didn't keep water from filling her shoes. Seconds later, already drenched, she rounded the curve and saw it.

"Yep, a house. Big, spooky house."

Lightning silhouetted a rambling, gabled structure with a wide porch.

"So it looks haunted. I don't care if it belongs to Dracula or the Bride of Frankenstein, as long as they have a phone."

Encouraged, she sloshed onward at a quicker pace. When she climbed the front steps and gratefully stepped under the porch roof, she noticed the house wasn't completely dark. Candlelight flickered in one of the windows.

Jane pounded on the door with a knocker shaped like a gargoyle. "Appropriate," she muttered.

Over the wind and rain she couldn't hear any movement inside, but a minute later the door opened. A slender woman approximately in her forties, with a severely trimmed cap of gray-streaked brown hair, stood on the threshold carrying a kerosene lamp. She gazed at Jane without any sign of surprise.

"My car crashed into a tree just up the road. If I could use your phone--"

"Do come in." The woman stepped aside and waved toward the dim interior. "The electricity is out, I'm sorry to say. That happens often here."

The door groaned when Jane closed it behind her. She stood dripping on the dark, polished wood floor of the foyer. An oval mirror on a coat rack showed her a drowned-rabbit reflection, and above the mirror a stuffed owl glared at her.

Obviously noticing Jane's dismay at the artifact, the woman said, "My father was an amateur taxidermist. I'm Adele Kendrick, by the way."

Jane introduced herself. "Sorry to bother you like this--"

"No trouble at all. I certainly wouldn't let you stay outside in that storm."

She led the way into the living room. Jane cringed at her own wet footprints on the Persian rug. More stuffed birds adorned every table, plus the mantle above the fireplace.

"The telephone might not work either, but you're welcome to try," Adele said, indicating a marble-footed end table.

The phone was a black, rotary-dial instrument the like of which Jane hadn't seen since childhood. Picking up the receiver, she heard nothing. "It's dead, all right."

"Typically, they won't get the utilities turned on until morning. You'll have to stay for the night."

"Oh, no, I couldn't put you to any trouble." She protested in the mildest possible tone, since she had nowhere else to go without walking miles through the downpour. She'd left the main highway out of a whimsical urge to explore the countryside. *That'll teach me*, she thought.

"No trouble. There's plenty of room, and I'll enjoy the company."

As Jane murmured her thanks, a framed picture next to the phone caught her eye. It portrayed a dark-haired man who looked somehow familiar.

"My twin brother Alan," said Adele. "He died sixteen years ago tonight." Her tone remained so cool that Jane didn't feel it would be appropriate to express sympathy. "It happened during a thunderstorm exactly like this." She picked up a pair of lighted candles. "Your room is this way."

Carrying the candles, Adele led Jane through the foyer and up a flight of stairs that creaked at every step. Shifting her eyes from the flickering shadows that kept pace with her, Jane wondered why her hostess insisted on offering a complete stranger a room in her house. *For all she knows, I could be an ax murderer.* A moose head mounted on the wall of the stair landing seemed to watch her with its gleaming eyes. With a tremor, she visualized herself in the same position.

She sternly ordered her imagination back into its cage. Adele wasn't Norman Bates, just a lonely woman who wanted company in the thunderstorm.

"Her" room smelled faintly of mildew. Not surprising, in such wet weather. Another Persian rug, like the one in the foyer, covered the floor. The dresser, bureau, and bed looked like cherrywood. A door led to an attached bath.

"This room hasn't been used in a long time, but it's the only one besides mine that has a bathroom. Make yourself comfortable while I get you something to wear."

Left alone with a single candle on the dresser, Jane took off her shoes, wrung out her hair, and dried her face with a towel hanging in the bathroom. It occurred to her that Adele kept this unused suite well supplied. Gazing at the dim glow of the candle in the mirror, she felt a breeze tickle the back of her neck and creep down her spine. When she reached up to finger her damp hair, the sensation vanished.

At the same moment, she thought she heard someone laughing. A man. Impossible--she and Adele were alone in the house. *Just the wind rattling the trees.*

She glanced at the dresser. One object sat in the center of the lace doily that covered the polished wood--a cedar jewelry box carved with a rose pattern. She couldn't resist touching the petals and leaves. The cedar fragrance drifted to her nose as if the wood were freshly cut. Idly toying with the lid, she found it locked.

At that moment Adele's knock came at the bedroom door. With a blush at the realization that she'd been snooping, Jane stepped away from the dresser and opened the door.

Adele carried a candle and a steaming mug, as well as garments draped over one arm. "I thought you might like some hot tea." She set down the candle and handed Jane a floor-length blue satin nightgown with a matching robe.

Jane accepted the nightclothes with a sense of awkwardness. They seemed too frivolous for a drenched traveler lost in a storm.

"What brings you here," Adele said, handing her the mug of tea, "if you don't mind my asking? It's a little off the beaten path."

Perched on the edge of the bed with a towel under her, Jane sipped from the cup. "My parents both died within the past year and left me--well, better off than I expected. I decided to travel around, see the country, while I thought about what to do next. I just finished touring Boston, and I got a sudden urge to explore the rest of Massachusetts."

"So you ended up here in the backwoods with a wrecked car." Adele smiled. "You probably wish you'd stayed on the freeway. Still, it must be nice to be able to follow your impulses." She walked to the window and gazed at the rain-spattered glass.

"I haven't gotten used to the freedom yet. My folks owned a store, and I've never done anything but work in the family business. They expected me to take over, which was the last thing I wanted. I sold it the first minute I could--so here I am."

Mention of the wreck reminded her of the man in the road, whom she'd almost forgotten in the past few minutes. She described him to Adele.

The other woman stepped away from the window and turned toward the mirror, fingering the jewelry box. "I wouldn't worry about it, if I were you. You couldn't have hit the man without noticing. And you didn't find any blood, much less a body, did you?"

"Well, no. But I still wonder what the heck he was doing out there."

Adele's sociable mood seemed to evaporate. "Don't let it bother you. I'm sure you need to rest." With a quick goodnight, she left the room, shutting the door behind her.

After bathing with what must have been the last of the hot water, Jane hung her wet clothes over the shower curtain rod and put on the satin nightgown. A ripple of air disturbed the humid atmosphere of the bathroom. She felt warmth on the nape of her neck, like a breath. When she gave her hair a nervous flick, something grazed her shoulder and glided down her back.

A hand--a hand patted her bottom.

She whirled around, wide-eyed, and faced an empty room. *Enough, I must be asleep standing up!*

She hurried to the bedroom, shed the robe, and scrambled under the covers. She didn't blow out the candle, though. With the thunderstorm still raging, she felt a need for the light.

Huddled under the sheets and quilt, she stared at the flame on the dresser. Bewildered, she saw another light take shape. Had she already lapsed into another dream? A neon blue glow surrounded the cedar box. It brightened, pulsed, elongated. Jane clutched the quilt up to her chin, watching the light expand into a column of blue flame. It flowed into a human shape and floated toward her. A pungent fragrance drowned out the faint whiff of mildew.

Old Spice aftershave.

The quilt snatched itself out of her hands and rolled to the foot of the bed. She made a grab for the sheet, but it whisked out of her reach, too. She tried to scream but only managed a squeak.

The six-foot-tall apparition coalesced into a man of about her own age, with dark hair that curled almost to his collar. If he'd worn a collar.

He didn't wear anything.

Jane crossed her arms over her chest and gibbered, "Go away--you're not real--this is a nightmare--"

"Nightmare?" His deep voice evoked a quiver in the pit of her stomach. "That's not very flattering." He sank into a sitting position on the end of the bed. "Please don't be afraid. I've been alone for so long."

She frowned at the man. He looked familiar. After a few seconds, she recognized him from the photo downstairs. "You're Adele's brother."

He nodded. "Alan."

The accident flashed into her mind. "Wait--I saw you outside, too. In the storm." She grabbed a pillow and swung it at him. It passed right through. "You idiot, you made me crash my car!"

He chuckled and tossed back the pillow. "That won't do any good. I can become solid or wraithlike at will." His voice softened. "I didn't take shape to fight with you, sweet Jane." He reached toward her.

She wedged herself against the headboard, drawing up her knees. She felt a tug at the hem of the nightgown. It lifted, allowing a swirl of air to tease her thighs. When she batted at the cloth to hold it down, it drifted upward on the other side.

"Stop that! What do you think you're doing?"

"I told you, I've been here alone a very long time."

A feather caress brushed her throat, circled each breast, and spiraled down her torso to the V of her legs. She blushed hotly at the awareness that her nipples had already peaked.

Her eyes involuntarily closed as a fresh cascade of sensations flooded her. "Please--"

"Please what? Leave you? Surely not." Warm lips touched her ear, then her throat. "I can't do you any harm. No pregnancy, no disease. I only want to share pleasure." His mouth tasted hers, and she opened to the probing of his tongue. "You want this, don't you? You've never had anyone of your own, have you?"

She struggled to resist the liquid warmth that suffused her. "What did you do, read my mind?" True, she'd never had a boyfriend for very long, since none of them lived up to her parents' standards.

"No, I don't have that power. I overheard your conversation with my sister. I had no trouble guessing that you're lonely, too."

The nightgown billowed up. Flickering tongue and caressing fingers explored her flesh until every inch tingled. Heat radiated along Jane's nerves. When she reached for him--whether to hug him or push him away, she wasn't sure--he swirled out of reach in a coruscation of light and a cascade of laughter.

Again a phantom tongue flicked her earlobe. Then he re-formed to sweep his hands down her body yet again.

What the heck, this is probably a dream, so why not enjoy it? She melted, and firm thrusts invaded her last defenses.

She abandoned all resistance and let herself drown in ecstasy. *It has to be a dream,* she told herself. *And if it isn't, I'll be gone tomorrow anyway.*

At last the whirlpool drew her into oblivion.

When she opened her eyes, she was alone in the room again. But the gown was bunched at her neck, and a breeze chilled her nude body. And she felt pleasantly sore in tender places.

She leaped out of bed and shrugged into the robe. Grabbing the candle, she scurried downstairs so fast that the flame dipped and sputtered. In a book-lined room off the foyer, she found her hostess reading by the kerosene lamp.

Adele looked up at Jane and tucked one hand under the flowing caftan. "I've been expecting you."

Jane stood in the doorway of the study, fighting to catch her breath. "You knew--that room's haunted--you knew all the time."

A slow nod. "Of course I knew. Certain talents run in our family. The so-called witches of Salem were innocent, but that doesn't mean there were no real ones in Massachusetts." She closed her book and set it aside. "That was Alan's bedroom from his fifteenth birthday to the night he died. Do sit down and stop making yourself hysterical. He didn't hurt you, did he?"

Jane felt her cheeks growing hot. "No," she murmured. In fact, given her limited romantic experience, the phantom was the best lover she'd ever had. Edging into the room, she took a seat in an armchair. "You said this was the anniversary of his death. How did it happen?"

"After our parents died, we--clashed--on many issues. Alan became engaged to a woman I disliked. She broke off the engagement because, as she put it, she didn't want to spend her life under the thumb of 'that bitch of a sister' of his." Adele's mouth tightened for a second before she drew a deep breath and went on. "We had a terrible fight, and Alan rushed out to his car. There was a thunderstorm, like tonight, and he was speeding. He was killed at the same curve where you crashed."

"How do you know--?"

"Because he always waits at that spot for a likely female to drive by. Every year on this same night."

"So that's why you had the room ready." Jane covered her eyes and waited for her head to stop spinning. "You're helping him lure women. Why?"

Adele raised her eyebrows in a restrained gesture of surprise. "Surely that should be obvious. To atone for what I did to him. This is the one night of the year he can materialize and enjoy the--pleasures--of the body. He makes love to them, a different one each year, and they leave the next morning convinced it was all a dream. He's searching for the right woman, the one who can bring him fulfillment. When he finds her, he'll be free of his present limitations and able to manifest whenever he chooses. The least I can do is smooth the way for him and not repeat my mistakes from the first time."

"And he hasn't found the 'right' person yet?"

Adele's eyes crawled over Jane's figure. "You may be the one. You're the first to understand that he's real. And you fit one other condition--nobody will miss you anytime soon."

"Now wait a minute!" Jane sprang to her feet. "You're crazy if you think I'm staying here another minute."

Still calm, Adele stood up. "Of course you're staying, as long as Alan wants you." The hand that she'd had hidden under her caftan emerged, holding a pistol. "Back to the bedroom, dear."

With her hands in the air, Jane marched upstairs ahead of her hostess. Since "You'll never get away with this" seemed dubious as well as trite, she didn't say it.

In the upstairs hall, Adele lifted the lamp to show a deadbolt attached to the outside of the doorjamb. "You see, I have everything prepared. Get inside."

Jane obeyed, walking over to sit on the tousled bed. Adele paused to caress the top of the cedar box. "Don't worry, dear, you'll have everything you need. I wouldn't think of mistreating my brother's lover."

"That box--" Its significance clicked into place in Jane's mind. "Don't tell me that's--"

"Yes, Alan's ashes. Our father believed in preserving things--you saw all those stuffed animals. I'm like him that way. I hang onto what's mine." She backed toward the door, with her aim never faltering. "Now, I do think you should get some rest."

After Jane heard the deadbolt snick into the locked position, she collapsed on the pillow and rubbed her eyes. "I don't believe this! I'm stuck in the Bates Motel with a ghost and a crazy lady."

A deep voice said, "Hey, I'm really sorry about this." The scent of Old Spice filled the air.

Jane's eyelids flew open. Alan stood beside the bed, looking completely solid--and still naked. She hastily tugged the quilt over her. "Yeah, sure you are. You brought me here in the first place."

"But I never told Adele to lock you in. You think I like this any better than you do?"

"You acted like you were having a good time a few minutes ago." She felt a blush spreading from her face over her entire body.

"Well, so did you." An insubstantial hand brushed her hair back from her forehead.

"Cut that out! And can't you conjure up some clothes?"

His bare skin morphed into jeans and a sport shirt. "I do want you, but not as a prisoner. This is just another way for that sister of mine to hold onto me for the rest of her life. You think I've never wanted to leave?"

"Why didn't you?"

"I can't move any farther from my ashes than the spot where I died. To get away from this house, I'd need a live person to transport my earthly remains to some other location."

Forgetting to cling to the quilt, she said, "You want me to get you out of here?"

"You'd be saving my--well, not my life, but I'd be eternally grateful." He sat on the edge of the mattress, which didn't sag.

"You're forgetting one thing. I'm locked in, and your sister has a gun."

"No problem." With a wave of his hand, he said, "Look in the closet." When she opened the closet door, Alan pointed to a discolored square of floorboard. "Pry that up."

The crude trapdoor revealed empty space between the floor and the ceiling below it. The hiding place held a coil of rope.

"Good," said Alan. "I figured Adele never found that. Our parents were the domineering type--like yours, I'll bet. I fixed a way to sneak out at night without getting hassled."

Jane pulled up the rope and discovered that it had a noose on one end and knots at one-foot intervals. "You expect me to climb out the window in this rain?"

"It's died down to a drizzle, and the thunder's stopped." Listening, she realized he was right. "It's still dark enough," he said, "that you have a good chance of getting away without Adele noticing."

"What happens if she does notice and comes after me?" Already Jane was stripping off the robe and nightgown, though. She wasn't likely to get a better chance of escape.

"Let me worry about that." His hands skimmed over her bare shoulders and circled around her waist to cup her breasts.

Exasperated by the ripple of pleasure that spread down her body, she stalked into the bathroom to gather her still-damp garments. "Keep your mind--or whatever--on the prison break." She closed the door, realizing the futility of the gesture a second too late, and tugged on her clothes. With a moment's pause to squelch her queasiness about touching it, she crammed the cedar box into her oversize purse, along with her flashlight.

After looping the rope's end around a bedpost and tightening it, she slung the purse strap over her shoulder, then dropped the makeshift ladder out the window. When she lowered herself over the sill and gripped the first knot, she decided she was glad it was too dark to see the ground. Better to creep down the wall one step at a time, with Alan's whispered instructions to guide her hands and feet. Thank heaven the wind had faded to a light breeze. Her fingers ached from clutching the rope. It felt like only twelve or fourteen hours before her canvas shoes touched the squishy grass.

"This way," Alan breathed in her ear, "to the road."

As soon as she had sloshed away from the house into the trees, she switched on the flashlight. A gust of wind made her shiver, from chill instead of delight this time. "This is the last time you'll catch me taking any local color side trips," she muttered.

Just when she caught sight of the pavement through a gap in the trees, the halo of another light appeared in front of her. It danced over the ground until it approached close enough for her to glimpse Adele carrying it.

Jane drew a breath to run.

"Don't," Alan said. "I'll take care of this."

With a dramatic whoosh of air, he materialized in Adele's path. Jane noticed that he wore his crash victim guise, blood streaming down his face and staining his shirt.

Adele froze with the flashlight in one hand and pistol in the other. "Good thing I decided to check on your girlfriend once more. I had a feeling she'd try to escape. Stop wasting my time, Alan. I can shoot her right through you."

"Lot of good that'll do any of us."

"You'll still have her, just not in physical form."

He loomed up, half again life-size, with blue flame crackling around him. "Listen here, Sis. If you try to stop us, or hurt her in any way, I'll make the rest of your life hell. You'll think you're in the middle of *The Exorcist, The Amityville Horror*, and *Poltergeist* all rolled into one."

Adele lowered the gun and retreated a pace. "You wouldn't."

"Oh, yeah? Remember the time I left Dad's stuffed rattlesnake under your pillow?"

"You were eleven years old!"

A limb broke off an enormous oak tree and crashed in front of her. "Right, and I've had plenty of time since to think up new tricks. How about when I showed your junior prom date your nude baby pictures?"

Adele's mouth sagged open.

"Or when I put green food color in your shampoo? Or hid that tape recorder in the wall behind your closet, playing 'Duke of Earl' in a continuous loop? Took you three hours to find it." He punctuated the sentence with an eerie chortle. "Hey, there's a thought. Now I could do that continuously for days. Wouldn't even need a tape deck."

Adele stumbled backward with a screech of alarm. "No--you wouldn't--all right, go! Leave and never come back! See how you like it out there!" She turned and ran toward the house.

Contracting into his normal shape, Alan lightly placed a hand on Jane's arm. "Come on, there's a gas station half a mile around the bend. We can get your car towed."

By the time they reached the blacktop, he'd thinned to a human-shaped wisp of fog.

"I've been thinking," Jane said. "We need some ground rules. For one thing, no spying on me when I don't know you're around."

"Would I do a thing like that?" came a hollow whisper.

"I don't know. That's why I'm telling you. If you want to materialize, you warn me you're doing it."

"Agreed."

"I like my independence," she said, matching the words to the rhythm of her brisk strides. "I'm not about to go from being dominated by my folks to being dominated by a ghost." She swatted away the flicker of his tongue at her right ear. "Not even a totally sexy one."

"Very well." A long sigh. "I understand."

"Make sure you do." She patted the bulge in her purse. "Because I'm in charge here. If you don't behave, I'll tie a brick to this box and throw it off a bridge, and you can have fun seducing the fish. Clear?"

"Perfectly clear, my love."

The End

You can find ALL our books on our website at:

http://www.writers-exchange.com

all our fantasy novels:

http://www.writers-exchange.com/category/genres/fantasy/

All our romances:

http://www.writers-exchange.com/category/genres/romance/

All Margaret's Books:

http://www.writers-exchange.com/Margaret-Carter/

About the Author

Marked for life by reading *Dracula* at the age of twelve, Margaret L. Carter specializes in the literature of fantasy and the supernatural, particularly vampires. She received degrees in English from the College of William and Mary, the University of Hawaii, and the University of California, with her dissertation published as *Specter or Delusion? The Supernatural in Gothic Fiction*. Her other works include *Dracula: The Vampire and the Critics*, *The Vampire In Literature: A Critical Bibliography*, and *Different Blood: The Vampire As Alien*. She is also the author of a werewolf novel, *Shadow Of The Beast*, and four vampire novels, *Dark Changeling* (2000 Eppie Award winner in Horror), *Child Of Twilight*, *Sealed In Blood*, and *Crimson Dreams*, along with a fantasy novel, *Wild Sorceress*, co-written by her husband Les Carter, and a horror novel, *From The Dark Places*.

Margaret and Les, a retired Navy Captain, have four sons and several grandchildren. For fans of "Vamp Tales", please do not hesitate to visit her website: The Vampire's Crypt at:

http://www.margaretlcarter.com/

You can keep track of all Margaret's books on her author page at Writers Exchange E-Publishing:

http://www.writers-exchange.com/Margaret-Carter/

If you enjoyed this author's book, then please place a review up at the site of purchase, and any social media sites you frequent!

If you want to read more about books by this author, they are listed on the following pages...

Crimson Dreams

The summer when Heather was eighteen, her dream beast's nightly visits warded off loneliness and swept her away in flights of ecstasy. Now, returning to the mountains to sell her dead parents' vacation cabin, she finds her "beast" again. But he turns out to be more than a dream. She meets Devin in the flesh, apparently not a day older. His first human lover, centuries in the past, died horribly because of her devotion to him. Does he dare expose another mortal woman to that risk?

Publisher: http://www.writers-exchange.com/Crimson-Dreams/

Passion in the Blood

Cordelia and her twin sister don't realize the mother who left them soon after their birth bequeathed them a dark bloodline. They're half vampire. Although human in most respects, they possess certain psychic gifts. A friend of their late father's, Karl, also a vampire, has been watching over their family for generations in honor of his love for their distant ancestor. When her sister is kidnapped and Cordelia must beg for help from Karl, she learns the truth about his vampirism and her own heritage. In the process, she and Karl form a blood bond that leads to deeper intimacy than either one could have anticipated.

Publisher: http://www.writers-exchange.com/Passion-in-the-Blood/

Different Blood: The Vampire as Alien

Different blood flows in their veins--but our blood quenches their thirst. From Bram Stoker's 1897 creation of Count Dracula, portrayed as a foreign invader bent on the conquest of England, the literary vampire has symbolized the Other, whether his or her otherness arises from racial, ethnic, sexual, or species difference. Even before the bloodsucking Martians of H. G. Wells' *War of the Worlds*, however, popular fiction contained a few vampires who were members of alien species rather than supernatural undead.

Even more intriguing than interplanetary invaders are humanoid and quasi-humanoid beings who have evolved to live on Earth among us, often camouflaged as our own kind. The boom in vampire fiction that began in the 1970s engendered a variety of "alien" vampires, many of them portrayed as sympathetic characters. The science fiction vampire is especially suited to the presentation of vampirism as morally neutral rather than inherently evil.

Different Blood surveys the literary vampire as alien, whether extraterrestrial or a different species evolved on Earth, from the mid-1800s to the 1990s, and analyzes the many uses to which science fiction and fantasy authors have put this theme. Their works explore issues of species, race, ecological responsibility, gender, eroticism, xenophobia, parasitism, symbiosis, intimacy, and the bridging of differences. An extensive bibliography lists dozens of novels and short stories on the "vampire as alien" theme, many of which are still in print.

Publisher: http://www.writers-exchange.com/Different-Blood/

From the Dark Places and Against the Dark Devourer

From the Dark Places

When Father Michel Emeric and Dr. Ray Benson warn young widow Kate Jacobs of occult danger stalking her, she dismisses them as deranged fanatics. The eerie disappearance of her four-year-old daughter, Sara, changes her mind. Ray and Father Mike rescue Kate's child, but the fight has only begun. Dark powers from beyond our world want to destroy Kate and Sara and prevent the birth of a future child foretold to have extraordinary psychic powers and a destiny as a great warrior against evil. Kate must develop her latent wild talents and allow Sara to do the same, in a universe weirder--and more dangerous-- than she's ever imagined.

Publisher: http://www.writers-exchange.com/From-the-Dark-Places/

Against the Dark Devourer (Sequel to From the Dark Places)

All her life, Deborah has known she and her older sister have extraordinary psi powers. When their mother dies suddenly, Deborah learns she's meant to use her gift against the forces of darkness in some special way. How, she doesn't have a clue, but she wants no part of this alleged fate. Yet with evil forces stalking her, can she avoid the battle ahead?

All his life, Victor has known he and his twin sister have a unique destiny. Bred to serve inhuman entities from another dimensional plane, he's instructed to either seduce a strange young woman who poses a grave threat to the cult he belongs to...or destroy her.

Unexpectedly, he finds Deborah not only attractive and intelligent but his equal in psychic power. Although his cult views religion with contempt--and she's an unabashed Christian--he's helplessly drawn to her. For her part,

Deborah finds in Victor a kindred spirit. For the first time, someone other than her sister can empathize with her differences from "normal" people. Is prophetic destiny written in stone, even for two potential foes falling in love? A paranormal romance inspired by C. S. Lewis's *That Hideous Strength* and the cosmic horror of H. P. Lovecraft.

Publisher: http://www.writers-exchange.com/Against-the-Dark-Devourer/

Hearts Desires and Dark Embraces

When Margaret L. Carter first read *Dracula* at the age of twelve, her spontaneous reaction was to wonder how the undead Count saw the events in which he was portrayed as the villain. She's always been fascinated with the "monster's" viewpoint and relationships between human and nonhuman beings. Most of the stories in this collection can be described as romances, and all involve love and passion in some form. Here you'll encounter vampires, elves, ghosts, and at least one human-monster hybrid. The vampire stories in the first half of the book are part of an ongoing series in which the creatures we know as vampires belong to a naturally evolved, nonhuman species secretly living among us. Readers can get better acquainted with them in *Crimson Dreams, Sealed in Blood,* and *Passion in the Blood.*

Publisher: http://www.writers-exchange.com/Hearts-Desires-and-Dark-Embraces/

Sealed in Blood

Science fiction conventions attract some strange people, but Sherri Hudson never expected to spend a con weekend helping a sexy man in a cape steal photos of a winged alien. When the photographer is murdered and Nigel Jamison reveals to Sherri that the "alien" is actually his sister, the situation gets intriguingly complicated. Unwillingly swept up in Nigel's quest to rescue his sister, Sherri can't help being fascinated with him. By the time she finds out he's a vampire, the fascination has become mutual--and too strong to resist.

Publisher: http://www.writers-exchange.com/sealed-in-blood/

Sealing the Dark Portal

Almost nothing Rina remembers about her life is true. Rather than the ordinary librarian she believes herself to be, she's actually a sorceress who fled from another world to ours when creatures from an alien dimension devastated her home and killed her family. Now they've pursued her to our world, summoned by a sorcerer who plans to open a portal and invite monstrous entities from the void between dimensions to overrun this planet. Rina's former bodyguard, a cat shapeshifter who was once her lover and still yearns for her, helps her true memories to awaken. She must come to terms with the truth about her past so that together they can save their new home from the fate of their old one.

Publisher: http://www.writers-exchange.com/sealing-the-dark-portal/

Shadow of the Beast

After the mysterious deaths of her brother and sister at the fangs of what looks like a feral dog, Jenny Cameron develops nightmares and blackouts. The quest for the truth about herself leads to her long-lost father, who deserted the family before her birth. He seeks redemption for the curse he carries, but has his bloody past condemned him beyond salvation? When Jenny discovers the secret of her dark heritage, she's no longer sure she can trust her dangerous nature enough to be with the man she loves, and she may ultimately be forced to destroy her own father. Fearing she has inherited the violence that rages in him, she struggles to find her true self under the shadow of the beast.

Publisher: http://www.writers-exchange.com/Shadow-of-the-Beast/

Wild Sorceress Series
By Margaret L. Carter and Leslie Roy Carter

In a world where hostile nations wield magic in combat, twin sorceresses separated at birth and brought up on opposing sides of the war find each other. Together, they face persecution for using wild magic, fight against traitors and assassins, explore family secrets, and discover the hidden origins of magic itself. Above all, to protect their world, they must deal with ancient, powerful dragons that most people don't even believe exist.

Prequel: Legacy of Magic

Most people in the country of Saphradea admire sorcerers and dream of having magical powers. Not Merina, a young woman who detests magic because she thinks it ruined the life of her mother, a failed sorceress candidate who abandoned her in infancy.

When Merina's fiance, Trinames, announces he's decided to go for training as a Healer sorcerer, her personal world turns upside down. Merina is heiress to a tract of rich farmland, and she wants only to manage her own property and bring up a family in peace--a dream she thought Trinames shared. Yet events conspire to force her into a realm of magic and intrigue she never wanted.

When Trinames is kidnapped and she strikes out across the wilderness to rescue him, in company with a wandering trader who turns out to be more than he appears, she runs into a crisis that awakens magical powers she shouldn't even possess.

Publisher: http://www.writers-exchange.com/Legacy-of-Magic/

Book 1: Wild Sorceress

In a world where warring nations use magic in combat, years ago young sorceress Aetria's untamed power caused a disaster on the battlefield. Temporarily banished and retrained, she's returned to the army to redeem herself as head of a company of novice mages. She uncovers a traitorous plot by her own commander, renews her bond with her "imaginary" childhood friend, and meets her long-lost twin sister. While also becoming a trusted friend of the commanding general of the army, Aetria unearths secrets of the true nature of the magic she and her comrades wield.

Publisher: http://www.writers-exchange.com/Wild-Sorceress/

Book 2: Besieged Adept

While learning to control her wild sorcery, Adept Aetria has defeated a pair of traitors trying to kill her, found a long-lost twin, and uncovered secrets of the source and nature of magic. Now she continues her research while battling the remnants of the Neo-Aggressor rebellion and integrating raw, untrained talent into the Sorcerer Corps. Meanwhile, she discovers deeper secrets of her own family background, along with a surprising new foe and a destiny she never dreamed of. Furthermore, she learns that her "imaginary" dragon friend Rajii actually exists...but so do less friendly dragons. What does their agenda mean for the future of humanity and magic in Aetria's world?

Publisher: http://www.writers-exchange.com/Besieged-Adept/

Book 3: Rogue Magess

Sorceresses Aetria and Coleni discover that both their own births and the history of their world have been manipulated in secret by an ancient, powerful race of dragons. Some, like Aetria's lifelong friend Rajii, have benevolent intentions toward humanity while others want to restore the people of the

Domains to total slavery. All, however, have their own agendas with human beings and mortal magic as pawns.

Emerging from their long-lost mother's hidden home in the deserted Non-Lands, Aetria and Coleni find themselves targeted by assassins under control of the dragons. While the sisters' powers continue to grow, so do the magical gifts of Coleni's baby daughter, but will their magic provide adequate protection?

Meanwhile, still viewed with suspicion for their "wild sorcery", they can't convince most of their rivals and allies, including Aetria's old mentor and the commanding general of the army, that the dragons and the danger they pose are real.

Publisher: http://www.writers-exchange.com/Rogue-Magess/

Series Page:

https://www.writers-exchange.com/wild-sorceress-series/

Windwalker's Mate

Shannon's little boy Daniel has disturbing psychic powers. He talks to the wind--and it listens. All Shannon wants is a normal life. She wants to forget the cult of the Windwalker, a dark god from another dimension, and the terrifying night when her child was conceived. But her first love, Nathan, son of the cult leader, contacts her for the first time since that horrific ceremony. He claims his father is stalking Shannon and Daniel. Whose child is Daniel, Nathan's or the Windwalker's? Nathan's father plans to use Daniel to open a gate between dimensions and unleash chaos on our world. To save her child and become reconciled with her first love, Shannon may have no choice but embrace the strange powers she previously rejected.

Publisher: http://www.writers-exchange.com/windwalkers-mate/

You can find ALL our books up on our website at:

http://www.writers-exchange.com

all our fantasy novels:

http://www.writers-exchange.com/category/genres/fantasy/

All our romances:

http://www.writers-exchange.com/category/genres/romance/